SWITCHBACK

SWITCHBACK

Susan Dunlap

This first world edition published 2015
in Great Britain and the USA by
SEVERN HOUSE PUBLISHERS LTD of
19 Cedar Road, Sutton, Surrey, England, SM2 5DA.
Trade paperback edition first published 2015
in Great Britain and the USA by
SEVERN HOUSE PUBLISHERS LTD.

British Library Cataloguing in Publication Data

Dunlap, Susan author.
  Switchback.
  1. Lott, Darcy (Fictitious character)–Fiction. 2. Zen
  Buddhists–California–San Francisco–Fiction.
  3. Detective and mystery stories.
  I. Title
  813.5'4-dc23

ISBN-13: 978-0-7278-8522-7 (cased)
ISBN-13: 978-1-84751-622-0 (trade paper)
ISBN-13: 978-1-78010-675-5 (ebook)

All Severn House titles are printed on acid-free paper.

Severn House Publishers support the Forest Stewardship Council™ [FSC™],
the leading international forest certification organisation. All our titles that
are printed on FSC certified paper carry the FSC logo.

Typeset by Palimpsest Book Production Ltd.,
Falkirk, Stirlingshire, Scotland.
Printed and bound in Great Britain by
TJ International, Padstow, Cornwall.

To Pat Priester McKeon

ACKNOWLEDGEMENTS

I am grateful to stuntwoman/stunt coordinator Carolyn Day, to my writing buddies Gillian Roberts, Susan Cox, Louise Ure, Linda Grant and Sarah Shankman. And, as always, my thanks go to my superb agent, Dominick Abel.

ONE

'**K**ill the Buddha,' Leo Garson, abbot of San Francisco's
Barbary Coast Zen Center said. *If you meet the Buddha in the road, kill the Buddha.*
I, Darcy Lott, his assistant, knew the koan. 'I have to
choose . . .'

We were in the *dokusan* room where he met formally with
students, sitting cross-legged on black two by three inch mats,
zabutans, set so close our knees nearly touched.

On a low altar, candlelight quivered by a ceramic Buddha.
The scent of sandalwood wrapped around us like a shawl
enclosing my question.

'. . . choose between . . .' I swallowed. 'How can I give up
what I can't live without?'

He might have smiled and said, 'You'll live.' Instead, he waited.

'I love stunt work, the choreographing, the high falls, the *feel*
of the air as I fly free. The *thwap* the catcher bag makes when
I hit it just right. And the car gags – when I hit the ramp just
right and roll the junker, and the whole crew explodes in cheers.
I love being a stunt double, doing the gags . . . I . . .'

I had to face reality. That's why I was sitting here. 'There's
no work in this city. San Francisco's too expensive to shoot in.
There aren't enough sound stages; last year's spaces have been
gobbled up by developers or tech companies. Movie companies
come with trailers, food trucks, trucks for lighting and equipment,
and, Leo, there's no parking! Not without pissing off the
neighbors.'

'Parking!' Leo laughed.

Despite everything, I did too, for a moment. 'I've hung
on because I love being back in the city. My family's here,
the *zendo*, you, my Zen practice. Being your assistant . . .
but . . .'

'But?'

'The longer I'm out of work, the rustier I look. Directors

wonder if there's something wrong with me. If they remember me at all.'

The roshi sat, hands resting one on the other, legs crossed. His eyes were lowered, his breathing undisturbed. He was neither pressing me nor offering escape. Beside him lay his *kotsu*, a polished S-shaped stick about eighteen inches long, given when his teacher granted him permission to teach. Like him, it was stronger and sturdier than it appeared. Like him, the wood had an odd homey quirk that always made me smile. Leo was just over fifty, with a shaved head and features too big for his face, but here in the dokusan room, in a black robe like the ones roshis have worn for centuries, he seemed ageless.

I said, 'If I want to be a stunt double I'm going to have to move to Toronto or somewhere where things are better.' I met his gaze and silently implored him to produce an answer I knew did not exist. 'I can't bear to leave.'

He let his gaze drop and sat totally still, his breath softly moving. I sat like a tornado in an opaque jar. At his monastery hours north of here he'd chosen me to be his assistant over more likely students. When he left there, he'd asked me to come with him to the city, to set up the Zen Center. I'd cracked my soul open to him. How could I ever leave?

But how could I face never again doing another stunt?

He picked up the kotsu, stopped and put it down. For a full half minute – an eternity in here – he didn't move at all. Then he reached over and touched my hand. 'There was a time I knew the right thing and I did it. I was wrong.'

'And?'

'Sometimes the "Buddha" you see is not the Buddha at all; it's just what you see. When you indulge your delusions, you create your own Buddha.' He moved his hand to his bell. 'If you meet the Buddha in the road, kill the Buddha.'

He rang the bell.

I sat, stunned. *I* wasn't through. Well, I hadn't thought I was through, but in his mind there was nothing more to say.

I could have grabbed his hand before it reached the bell. Traditionally a student has that right to demand more, but when a roshi rings the bell it means figure it out yourself. You *can* figure it out. In the case of me, who lived upstairs in the room across the hall from Leo, demanding elucidation would have been a little disrespectful and just plain embarrassing.

And it wouldn't have mattered. This interview was over. He'd made his point, given his teaching. The koan was well known. Discard your attachments. Let go of the things you can't bear to give up. Do not be caught even by your image of your Zen practice, of enlightenment, of the Buddha. Both of your choices are false Buddhas.

I bowed to Garson-roshi and he returned the bow, palms together, our torsos bending slightly forward till we stopped inches apart, in that moment *not one, not two*.

I turned back around, lifted myself from the cushion, plumped it, stood and bowed again and backed out into the hall.

I stood for a moment preparatory to shutting the door on the roshi, the interview, the comfort of indecision. The candle beside Leo flickered in the dim overhead light. The incense had burned down to half an inch, its smoke curling toward me at the open door. I—

Someone shoved past me.

Into the dokusan room.

Shouting.

I heard Leo's voice, ridiculously calm.

The intruder was screaming.

'Don't—' Leo groaned.

All of it in a breath's time.

The attacker grabbed the kotsu beside Leo's leg and swung it up overhead, holding it in both hands like an axe, like the Grim Reaper.

For an instant, nothing moved. The candlelight glowed off the thick, dark-buffed wood. It threw his black hoodie and loose pants into shadow. The incense smelled like fire, like ash.

Then everything moved. Arms drawn back over the shoulder; weight shifted, then fast movement forward. He was going for Leo, his back rounded, his arms flying forward.

I flung myself at him. He was thin, weedy. Still, I couldn't get him down. Arms hammering. Crack of wood on . . . something. Screams.

Arms around him, I threw my weight backwards. My hands were slipping. I didn't dare let go.

The guy was hitting, thrashing like he had eight arms. His feet slipped like skates. I was falling back, almost in slow motion. I hit the floor with a crack. He came down on top of me and knocked my breath out. Gasping, I grabbed his neck. He yelped and twisted free. As he staggered toward the doorway I kicked with both feet. He stumbled, one knee on the floor, the other foot slipping. I rolled up on my knees, threw myself at him, shoved him over the sill and slammed the door shut.

I braced myself against the door, my whole body rocking as I panted. The candle lay on the floor, its flame out. Nothing burned. The little Wedgewood vase was on its side, water spilled in an ellipses of sorts. The Buddha lay in pieces. I noted all that in an instant before I looked at Leo.

'Omigod!'

Leo was still sitting, his legs in the lotus position, left foot on right thigh, right foot on left: the position monks have sat in for thousands of years, in which they could fall asleep and not fall over. Leo had not fallen over. But his face was covered in blood. It ran over his eyes. I couldn't even see his eyes. Couldn't make out his nose and mouth. Blood was dripping onto his black robe, turning it a murky brown.

'Omigod, Leo!'

He didn't move.

I was still bracing myself against the door. I forced myself to stay put, to listen through the thrusts of his breaths and of mine for noise outside. Was the guy in the hoodie still there, ready to burst back in? The door was flimsy, closer to a curtain than a barricade; it opened inward. If he flying-wedged into it, there'd be no way to keep him out. Leo's teaching stick . . . but no, I couldn't even use that. Hoodie still had it. He could attack Leo with it, again.

Footsteps? Thud of shoes on wood? Groaning, yelling? Nothing. The only sounds I could be sure of were Leo's breaths – short, thick.

'Leo, are you OK?'

He tried to speak. I couldn't make out the words.

Letting go of the door, I bent down and pulled out tissues one after another from the pale blue box near him, dunked them in the water bowl on the altar and put them in Leo's hand. 'Here. For your eyes. Be careful.'

Yanking out another, I said, 'Do you have blood in your mouth? Here, spit into this!'

I dunked some more, blotted the blood on his forehead. He was holding his tissues over his eyes. Was he cut? I couldn't tell. Concussion? Worse? Head wounds bleed a lot. And he was bleeding *a lot*. Already the tissues were soaked. 'I've got to call the medics. Got to go to the phone. Can you hang on?'

'Mm, OK.'

I opened the door, peered out into the hallway. No sign of the assailant. Then I ran for the phone. The landline, in the hall upstairs. Eternity passed while it rang, and another eternity while I told them a man had been beaten, had head wounds and was bleeding hard. While I repeated the address I was stretching the cord down the stairs around the landing, staring down the bottom flight at Leo's open door, at the closed door to the courtyard, poised to leap if the guy came running back in. 'Don't hang up,' the dispatcher said. I didn't. I let the phone dangle as she launched into the safety questions. I took the steps back down in two bounds, then raced into the dokusan room, terrified that I'd find Leo unconscious.

He was still sitting, his crossed legs holding him vertical, his hand frighteningly loose on the tissues. I eased him on to his back, hoping that lying flat was the right thing, not the absolutely wrong thing.

I wiped his bloody eyes again, covered them with fresh wet tissues then raced back upstairs. I had to take a deep breath before I could trust myself not to yell into the phone. 'The medics – where are they? His head's covered in blood.'

And then I heard the sirens.

And brakes squealing, horns blaring—

And the crash.

TWO

The ambulance? Crashed? How long could Leo hold on? His face was still covered in blood!

I raced out the zendo door into the courtyard, expecting to see a heap of crumpled red metal in the road and hear firefighters and EMTs barking orders into phones. But Pacific Avenue was its normal, still self. Boutiques and small law offices, closed and dark, no moving cars, no vacant curbs. Fog was blowing in from the west, covering the remnants of the daylight sky.

Then, abruptly, sirens burst the air from all directions. On Columbus Avenue, the major street by the corner of our minor street, people were running, yelling, like it was a bad night in Hell. But wherever the action was, it wasn't visible from here. From the zendo courtyard I couldn't see broken glass, crunched metal, rubble or even flames. And not a single emergency medical van.

Where are the paramedics for Leo? Was this fracas blocking them? It was rush hour. Would this blockage spread to all the surrounding streets?

'Stop!' I said aloud to myself. *Focus!*

I'm a stunt double – I don't show panic. *Outwardly cool* was my mantra when a gag went bad, a friend cracked an ankle or a neck. But Leo . . .

Outwardly cool, dammit. For Leo. I made myself walk, not race, back inside.

Leo was ashen under the blood blotches splattered over his face. He looked like his skin was sinking into his bones, while bruises were growing on his cheekbones and his forehead. His nose was surely broken. His eyelids looked like mahogany mushrooms; his eyes nearly squeezed closed.

I knelt down next to him and put a hand on his. 'Leo' – my voice sounded exponentially more controlled than I felt – 'how are you feeling?'

'Feeling.' Normally his voice had a firm tenor quality; now it was frayed and barely audible. *Feeling* was what he was doing. Just feeling. Only that. Not, like me, worrying.

Still, I wanted to . . . I wanted to bring him tea, fluff the mats under him, fan him, warm him, make him more comfortable. I don't know what. Make him safe. I said, 'I need to keep an eye out for the ambulance. I'll be right back. Will you be OK without me?'

'Don't worry.' He meant, I knew, not to indulge in the delusion of worry, of made-up possibilities. Not to be somewhere other than in the reality of this moment.

I walked, not ran – I can walk fast – back into the courtyard. No ambulance. Fog already thicker. The dusk wind that slices east through the streets colder. Sirens rising and falling, muffled by distance and fog. Red lights shone at the corner on Columbus but none was moving. I hurried back inside and squatted down next to Leo as he bled out all his color. I felt like I was fracturing.

And then I inhaled, felt my ribs moving and listened to the sound of my breathing in and out. In a minute the swarm buzzing around my head lifted just a bit, as if I had taken a step back from the turmoil. Leo didn't look any better; help wasn't any nearer.

Should I call 911 again? Go back to the landline upstairs? The dispatcher – the dispatcher! Was she still on the line? Taking the stairs two at a time, I grabbed the phone as I hit the landing and shouted into it: 'The paramedics? Where are they?'

Before she could answer, the siren broke off. Brakes shrieked. Leather slapped on the sidewalk. I guided the paramedics inside and suddenly the little interview room was bulging with people and equipment. A gurney appeared; paramedics braced Leo's neck, scooped him onto a tray and the tray onto the gurney. For a moment, his lips quivered. I thought he was going to speak, to say something about the tray, something light, like he might be mistaken for a Thanksgiving turkey. Say *something* to me.

His eyes shut, his head fell back and the paramedics seemed to double their speed. They didn't pause to ask if I wanted to ride with him.

The ambulance siren'd off and I stood on the sidewalk not

even knowing where it was headed. No one to be outwardly cool for. All the panic I'd kept leashed in burst forth. My hands were shaking, fluttering against my legs; my breath moved in useless little chugs.

I didn't notice the cop till he spoke. 'Are you related to Mr Garson?'

Mr Garson? Like he was a supervising clerk in some county office?

'Wife? Domestic partner?' He was stocky but not fat, round-faced with a shaven pate stubbled with brown and gray. Mid-forties – old for a uniformed cop, like he'd joined the force after another career. Or he'd been busted back to patrol.

'He's the abbot here. I'm his assistant. You're taking me to the hospital, right, Officer . . .?'

'Snell.'

Snell? I'd heard that name before. Why? 'Let me grab my phone and wallet and lock the door.'

I couldn't have been gone more than ninety seconds, but it was enough time for him to check messages, make a call, whatever. He said, 'You're Lott's sister, huh?' with an edge to his voice that I'd heard all too often from other cops who knew my recently retired oldest brother. This wary tone could have come from any of John's fellow sworn officers whom he'd chewed out, turned in, gotten suspended, fired, indicted, or who just found him a pain in the ass.

'SF General?' I prodded. *Are they taking Leo to the San Francisco General trauma unit?*

'You witness the attack?'

'I'll answer your questions at the hospital.'

'I'm afraid, Ms Lott—'

As in, fat chance.

I could have argued. *Feel free,* he'd say. *We get paid by the hour.* I sighed and said, 'Let me speed things up for you, Officer Snell. I'm Darcy Lott. This is the Barbary Coast Zen Center. The ground floor has the meditation hall, the interview room, a tiny kitchen and toilet. I live upstairs, across the hall from Leo Garson. So, there are two rooms and bathroom up there. We have two *zazen* – meditation – sittings a day, Monday through Friday. Two days a week, during the afternoon sitting, Garson-roshi – that's

what we call our teacher, the roshi is a term of esteem that we
– his students, I mean, give him. Garson-roshi, see?'

Snell didn't see, didn't care.

I continued: 'Twice a week, mornings, and in the afternoons
after zazen, he offers private interviews in the room in which he
was attacked.' I had to take a long breath to maintain outwardly
cool.

Snell was focused on his notepad like the universe depended
on each blot of ink. Didn't the San Francisco Police Department
have computers or iPads or something more up-to-date than paper
and pen? Maybe Snell just couldn't be parted from his paper and
graphite security blanket.

I took another breath and described the attack in more detail
than I ever wanted to think about again. 'The attacker – I can't
tell you whether it was a man or a woman.'

For the first time he looked up skeptically. 'Try.'

I tried. 'They wore a hoodie. I only had contact with their
shins.' I tried to pull up the feel of those legs. 'Not a woman
who wears high heels. Not that shape of calf. But a runner, even
a walker . . . Could be a woman. Mid-height. Never spoke.'

'Rushed in, attacked Mr Garson and didn't say anything?'

'No. Shoved past me . . . OK, here's what it seems like now,
like he wasn't expecting a second person, just assuming he'd
find Leo, find Garson-roshi. So finding me in the hall, right
outside the interview room unnerved him. Big time. Maybe he
thought about turning and running. But then, maybe, and this is
just a guess – he saw Leo's kotsu—'

'His what?'

'A stick, but a thick one. Polished. Eighteen or so inches. It's
a sign of a teacher. Old-time teachers in China and Japan would
hit students with it to' – how could I explain this to him? – 'to
make them focus on that moment.'

'Bet that worked.'

Sarcasm? More than I'd expected from him.

Snell seemed equally surprised by his comment, as if the words
had popped out of a trapdoor in his head. He cleared his throat,
looked hard at his notepad.

'Leo had the kotsu beside his leg, near the middle of the room,
visible from the door.'

'So you're thinking it was a crime of opportunity.'

'I'm just saying.' *Saying too much. A chatty witness is a stupid witness.* That one from my brother Gary, the attorney. In his lexicon the only words spoken to the police should be I'm calling my lawyer. Still, the sooner SFPD found Leo's assailant the better all around.

'And then, Ms Lott?'

'The attacker ran.'

'You see where he went?'

'Out. Out of the building.'

'And then where? Which direction? Did you see that?'

'No, dammit! I had Leo to worry about. Leo, bleeding!'

'Leo? The abbot you live with.'

Yeah, that one. 'Yes.'

Behind him two beat cops and a plainclothes detective huddled by the zendo door. Snell nodded to me and sidled off, as if from one ominous dark puddle to another. The man made me think of a shelter dog.

A UPS truck rattled down the street like a brown marimba racing against the February dark and groaned to a stop at Columbus. I thought I could hear the bubble *op-op-op* of the ambulance speeding Leo to the emergency unit, but more likely it was from the crash on Columbus.

Ten minutes had passed and I wasn't at the hospital running interference for Leo. Leo was slight, but under those black robes or the sweats he wore around here he was a tough middle-aged fellow. If the assailant had gone for anything other than his head he'd probably be fine. Still, he needed someone there with him. The last thing I wanted was to have to call one of my siblings to help, have them tell the rest of the family there'd been an attack where their youngest sister lived and I was paying the ongoing price.

'Not any more,' the plainclothes cop was saying. He was laughing! 'Before he retired . . .' He spotted me and lowered his voice. But sotto voce clearly wasn't his style and his volume rose steadily till I heard, 'Yeah, he's her problem now.'

My problem.

I had the feeling he wasn't bothering to hide his laugh. There was a time when I could have dropped the name of Detective

John Lott and gotten a free pass. Then my concern would have been whether a specific cop hated him or feared him. Now that John had retired, no one feared him. There was only one option left. And being John Lott's sister had only one side – down.

The detective said something else and Snell strode back to me. I answered questions I'd already answered more than once. Another ten minutes shot. When Snell finally pulled open the patrol car's back door and motioned me into the cage I didn't comment that it was preferable to sharing a seat with him.

But I couldn't stop myself from saying, 'How about the siren?'

He pulled away from the curb, hung a U and headed the wrong way on the one-way street to the corner. It was just after seven; the sky heavy with the promise of rain. Buildings looked damp, the reds and whites of headlights and flashers shimmering across them. Traffic was still snailing. The ambulance with its lights and siren would be 'brushing road,' clearing traffic to the sides. But far ahead as it was, it wouldn't help us. It was probably already at the ER door. We needed to *move*! Lights, siren and speed. 'How about code three?'

'You *are* Lott's sister. But, listen, we got rules.'

'John's not a rule breaker.' *Do not get into this! Not John and the department.*

'No, he is not.'

I couldn't read Snell's tone: approving or sneering or just – I should be so fortunate – not getting into it.

'You live in the Buddhist place there? The two of you?'

'Yeah, upstairs, like I said. Not together. Are you going to use the siren?' I said in exactly the same tone as my brother, but I didn't care. Like, I suppose, John hadn't cared.

Snell started to make some comment. Then he caught himself and hit the siren instead and the flashers, leaned forward and stepped on the gas.

Ahead, a line of freeway hopeful vehicles idled two blocks from the entrance. Snell cut into the oncoming turn lane, sweeping away the cars ahead right and left with his flashers. Drivers jerked toward adjoining lanes, frantically trying to squeeze into spaces that didn't exist. Snell threaded through to the corner, shot straight across the intersection and into the next oncoming lane, sweeping away a new set of cars, trucks and two motorcycles like he was

a tsunami. My feet were braced, my hands against the back of
his seat, my arms ready to protect my neck if he crashed. I'd
been with John and I'd braced myself then. I trusted him. But
Snell? Who knew? He could be as good as John or he could
have Code 3 Delusion, in which the driver assumes the lights
and flasher throw a shield over him that will protect against all
vehicles in all forms in all places. I've done my share of car
gags; I've rolled cars, exploded them, driven them between
oncoming trucks and over cliffs – small cliffs. I hate driving with
amateurs. And Snell? He could have killed us six ways a minute.

I thought about Leo's face draining color like he was a sieve.
I kept silent, and hoped.

Face steeled in outwardly cool, I was ready for Snell's glance
in the rearview to see how much he'd scared Lott's little sister.
He did it just as he was turning on the freeway.

Even this late, 101 was crowded. Around San Francisco, rush
hour has become rush day. Now it was thick with techies who'd
lost track of time, clerks commandeered into unpaid overtime,
city workers anxious to get out of the city they couldn't afford
to live in. Cars moved close together but they moved fast.

We pulled off at Cesar Chavez, buzzed a couple red lights and
swung into the ER just behind the ambulance. I couldn't believe
it. 'Let me out!'

The medics were racing a gurney through the doors as Snell
released the lock and I leapt out and ran to catch up with Leo.

Of course, it wasn't him. The body on the gurney was an
African-American woman.

Too much time had passed. Surely Leo was already inside,
behind the double doors.

A guard blocked me. 'You can't go in there.'

I knew that, really. 'How can I find out—'

'The doctor will come out when he's done.'

I knew that, too. I checked with the admitting desk, badgered
Snell about pulling rank which he either didn't have or had no
intention of using. If he'd been John . . . But he wasn't.

There was nothing to do but sit here in this room of barely
contained panic and wait. Wonder about concussion, brain
damage, paralysis. Try not, as Leo would tell me, to mentally
replay the attack with a better outcome.

Sirens screamed and burbled to stops. Engines roared and slowed. Ambulances disgorged gurneys and paramedics to race and rattle through the double doors to the ER. San Francisco General is the trauma center for the city and the citizens were keeping it in business with families arriving, huddling in clumps, crying, yelling at each other, shouting over the noise into the phone to repeat again and again that Dirk had been hit by a bus, yes, in his new car, that Shane had been shot, Mom squashed by dump truck in the crosswalk on Market Street. Sounds banged off the walls. It was like an eight-plex cinema of tragedies.

I found a seat. Sitting, watching the seconds extend themselves as if nourished by the fear, I was almost grateful for the diversion of Snell's cowboy driving.

Snell settled himself next to me. Sadly, he was one of the freckled Irish whose pale skin was not improved by exposing previously protected regions, like his pate, to the sun. With hair, he might have been appealing. His features were chiseled, his eyes a pale blue, but fronting the great ball of bald, his face seemed like an afterthought. Like a spit of gum on a bongo.

'Thanks for driving me,' I said, 'but I'll be OK. You don't have to stay with me.'

'No, I do. Till one of the new detectives gets here.'

'But—'

Snell turned full face to me. He clenched his fist on this thigh and pressed. The indentations were clear on his pant leg. 'You could be back at your Zen place, waiting for your statement to be typed up. Or at the station waiting for the detective.'

'Even so—'

He lowered his voice. 'I stuck my neck out for you.'

'For the friend of an assault victim? The very worried friend. The friend who was in the room and . . .'

Oh, shit! The friend who was the only witness to an assault by a stranger she couldn't even identify by gender.

The friend who lived in the building with the victim.

The unmarried female who lived there with the male victim.

Snell had done me a favor. John Lott couldn't have done better. I said, 'Thanks.'

I was considering whether to ask why or just be grateful when the outer doors sprang open. A gurney sped through. Then another with a paramedic supporting an IV. And a third.

The entire waiting room crowd perked up. Questions bubbled. House fire? Minibus crash? Big accident scene?

'Columbus Avenue,' a woman called out. She was eyeing her phone. 'Multi-car pile-up. Hit and run.'

Columbus! I moved in front of her. 'Does it say any more? About the victims?'

'Let me see here.' She scrolled down, lost the page, reloaded it.

By the time she found the report again it was no surprise. 'Victim came running out of a side street into traffic. A Mazda hit him. Couldn't stop in time. Second victim was the driver. Third – on foot, just trying to get across the street.'

I grabbed Snell. 'Number one – that's him!'

THREE

The doors had swung shut, the gurney and paramedics inhaled into the hospital innards. Snell was staring after them. 'That's who?'

'That's the one who attacked Leo! The patient on one of those gurneys.'

'The man you didn't see well enough to describe? In the hoodie? The one you're not sure is a man or a woman?'

'Yes! You're a cop, go after him! Before he's swallowed up in there.'

'Just calm down!'

As one, Snell and I turned to the speaker. It was hard to say which of us was less surprised. Snell because he'd been talking about him, or me because in any bad situation it's just a matter of time till my brother John shows up and manages to irritate everyone involved, which he'd just managed to do. *Calm down!* Had those words, ever, in the history of humanity, calmed anyone? Had they not enraged anyone?

'John, we're losing the attacker!' I eyed Snell. 'Go!'

'You're not going anywhere till I know what's happening.'

Snell eased half a step back.

'So, Darcy, just what is this business?'

I gave him a quick rundown. I didn't waste time asking how he heard about the assault or discovered where we were. After thirty years on the force he was thick with sources. 'And the guy—'

'Or woman—' Snell put in.

'—who attacked Leo was just wheeled inside here. Officer Snell was headed to ID him.'

'Why are you still standing here?' John barked.

'Sorry, sir, but my orders are to stay with Ms Lott.'

'I've got her.'

Snell looked at his feet. He didn't actually shuffle, but came as close as possible without moving his shoes. 'I'm sorry, sir, but my orders . . .'

'*I* am ordering you to go.'

'Sorry, sir, but aren't you retired?'

'Don't you—'

'Officer,' I said, 'I will stay in this spot until you come back. There could be an earthquake and I'd still be here, under the rubble, waiting for you. Being lectured by my brother.'

No response.

'Or John can call your superior – right, John? – if that will smooth things.'

Still Snell hesitated.

A woman behind him leaned in closer. 'Go, you little . . .'

'Go! Go! Go!' a toddler chimed. He started to clap. 'Go!'

Snell pushed through the swinging doors.

John put his arm around my shoulder so we were side to side, close. Way too close. He walked us to the window. 'You can't stay in that place. I'll take you home.'

That place, i.e. the Zen Center. 'I'm fine.'

'Hardly. Garson runs that place like an all-night diner. Come. Go. No questions asked.'

'Hey, we have hours.'

'A couple of pimps go knives-out after each other in your courtyard—'

'Once! Only once.' And, boy, were we sorry about that. Leo and I dealt with the cops and reporters till dawn. John was still chewing on it. 'It happened once, weeks ago. In the middle of the night. We're careful. We have set zazen hours and Leo locks the doors other times.'

'And still, Darcy, a mad man races in and clobbers him. With his own stick. What kind of idiot keeps a stick by his side for anyone to grab?'

'A patrolman?'

Behind us a couple guys laughed. John shot them a look. They stopped. 'The point is,' he said at slightly nearer to normal volume, 'you're asking for trouble.'

'I'm staying.' I could have explained that there were still periods of zazen scheduled morning and afternoons and I had to be there. The students who sat then would be desperate to know how Leo was. Our stalwart friend, Renzo, at Renzo's Caffe on the corner, would be frantic. Plus . . . But none of that would matter to John. Fifty–fifty he wouldn't even be listening.

'Mom won't—'

'Don't even think of involving Mom!'

He stared. Mine was, I realized, a tone he'd almost never heard from me.

'Look, John, forget about me. You've got a crazed person running loose, or more to the point who was running loose and is now in this hospital. We don't know if he targeted Leo or if Leo was his flavor of the day. He could be eyeing the Bishop of San Francisco tomorrow, if he's out of here by then.'

'He'll be in jail tomorrow.'

'How? I can't ID him. Leo? Maybe. If he looked up before he was struck.' I could see his bloody face again, his eyes swelling shut.

'Try.' John motioned me to an empty bank of chairs against the wall. We took the middle two. 'Eyes shut. Picture him. Or – Jesus! – her.'

In a few minutes Snell would be back with his details and we'd both know. But anything I could remember before would strengthen the case against him. Or her.

John always contended that if you ask five witnesses in a bank robbery to describe the robber, you'll be lucky if they all agree on his sex. One Christmas when I was eight or nine he gave me a flash card set with Hollywood-ish perp pictures. The box said the point was to match the face to a name, but John's rules were to describe the face on the card so your teammate could pick it out of the pack. We all played it that night, three of us per team, and a couple of times after. We might have liked it but really no one can get into a game when the game-giver's snide about how poorly you're doing.

Body on the gurney? I wasn't going to win points for that.

John's game had a one-minute timer, loudly ticking off your seconds to failure. A bad description within the time limit was better than an inability to come up with anything. That, John suspected rightly, was a sign of the cardinal sin of slacking.

Eyes still shut, I tried to stop-frame the assailant in the dokusan room, to separate him from the fear and anger and worry that turned my memory into a blur of sick yellows. I tried it all again referring to him as 'her,' hoping either for a bingo or a dead stop that would tell me a female was a no-go.

But that was it. I didn't dare go over the images again lest I start adjusting my memories. In a few minutes, an hour, maybe when I saw him in a line-up at the station, I'd see how well I'd done.

But why had the assailant run out of the zendo so frantically? I tried to flash still frames of his run on my memory. He wasn't a runner, that was for sure. He moved fast; he was thin, narrow, but his feet . . . That's what I remembered – his feet in those green Crocs.

'Green Crocs!'

My brother glared at me.

'You know, those wide rubber shoes with the holes in them? People use them for gardening. Not around here, but in places where people have lawns and shrubs and flowers not in pots. You can slip them on.'

'The guy sloshed out in rubber slippers and you couldn't catch him? You go to all those exercise classes and—'

'Hey, Leo was bleeding. He probably had a concussion. I—'

The swinging doors opened out. Snell stalked back into the waiting room, looked from me to John and sighed. 'Gone,' he said.

'Who's gone?' John demanded.

'Accident victims.'

'Victims, plural?'

'Yeah, plural. Medic stashed them in the hall. They took the opportunity to depart.'

'They?' I asked with a sinking feeling.

'Victim number one, the runner. Vic number three, the pedestrian.'

'One male, one female?'

'Yes.'

'Paramedics roll in three accident victims and two of them walk out?'

Behind me a man said, 'No insurance.'

'Yeah, what they come after you for that fancy ride, you could pay rent for a month, honey.'

A general murmur rose around the speakers like the bread of complaint rising.

I remembered hearing the metal hitting metal, the sirens, noting the lights on Columbus. The whole scene I could never see. So, the guy went from bludgeoning Leo to causing a crash. He was getting to be a city-wide disaster in one body. 'Well, what's his name?'

'Not the one he gave, that much they do know.'

John inhaled theatrically, preparatory, I knew, to an icy mistral of sarcasm. 'Did they at least discern which patient was which gender?'

Snell just shook his head.

I thought John would have a good long chew on that, and me. But Snell was making him a tastier meal. 'The man who stabbed the abbot, you don't know who he is, and now he's disappeared.'

Snell let a beat pass. 'We don't know his identity, sir, or his whereabouts, or if he attacked Mr Garson. For that, we have only Ms Lott's word.'

'The remaining victim, Snell, do you have an ID?'

'No, sir.'

'Find out. Now!'

Snell whipped through the doors so fast he nearly decapitated a nurse.

'Thanks,' I muttered. John pretended not to hear. 'You think Snell'll find out?'

'Probably. But get a statement? Not a chance. Tomorrow at the earliest.'

'Then why'd you just about fling him in there?'

Facing me now, he put a hand on my shoulder – the 'I'm telling you for your own good' move. 'I know how these things go. Snell starts the search. He questions people, they brush him off, it gets his dander up. He's not about to wander back out here with his tail between his legs, right? So he keeps at it. He gets a nibble, a name. So now he's got something. *His* find. The person who can lead him to the person who attacked Garson. To the person who is not you! Now he's on the case, he's committed. Now you've got a bit of an ally. Not all the way, nowhere near, but more than he was when he was cooling his heels out here.'

Maybe. Or maybe Snell took his chance to be clear of both of us, walked back inside, climbed into an empty bed and pulled the sheet over his head. Probably not, though, from the I-hate-hospitals look on his face.

'Snell's got to be the weirdest cop I've ever met. And I'm including you in the "met" group.'

John chuckled. 'Snell? I heard something about him. Can't pull it up.'

'He's like a shelter dog.'

'Feel free to pass that on to him.'

I smiled. John's not entirely without humor, though in our family so much of it was at his expense that he rarely got to enjoy the payoff. I was about to ask where he'd learned that *his find* maneuver when he re-launched the 'Zen Center isn't Safe' spiel, which he interspersed with trips to the desk to hector the clerks about Leo's evaluation.

When the doctor finally – finally! – emerged from the double doors we were both relieved. Snell followed him.

He was a tall, narrow man with a high nose and startlingly pale eyes. Next to him John looked stubby and exceedingly white. 'I apologize for the delay. I was called to an emergency. A second emergency, you see.' His accent was lush and so thick that I felt like I was disassembling and rebuilding each noun and verb. His dark face was shadowed by darker circles under his eyes. He looked like he was dangling at the end of his way-too-long shift. Like they'd sucked out his innards to infuse the patient.

'Leo Garson?' I prompted.

'Mr Garson is in recovery.'

'And?'

'Mr Garson was fortunate. Half an inch medial—'

'Nearer?'

He nodded, but his focus was on John. Because he was the man, or even in plain clothes he exuded *police*? 'To his eye and there could have been problems, very serious problems.'

'But there weren't?' I said.

'No. He was fortunate.'

'His eyesight's OK?'

'The prognosis is positive. For the eye.'

My heart dropped into my gut. 'But?'

'The zygomatic process shows bruising.'

'The cheekbone?'

'As I stated, the patient was fortunate.'

'And?' I prodded.

'Broken left first metacarpal.'

'Broken thumb?' That's all? Broken hands and sprained wrists were rites of passage in the stunt world. John was staring at me. I couldn't tell whether he was amazed by how many medical terms I'd learned in my years of stunt mishaps or appalled.

'Concussion.'

I nodded, relieved. Another rite.

'What about his recall of the incident?'

The doctor nodded. 'Often in the case of assault there is no memory of the incident itself. But sometimes yes.'

'You don't know.' John's sarcasm was so muted only I caught it.

'Just so. We will be keeping him under observation for two days – three, perhaps.'

'That serious?' I asked.

'Yes.'

'Can I see him?'

'Yes.' The doctor nodded.

'No!' said Snell.

FOUR

'What do you mean "No?"' I glared at Officer Snell. 'Until and unless you are cleared, you are not to be within a hundred feet of Mr Garson.'

'So, clear me.'

'It's not my—'

'Get someone who can!'

'Those were my orders.' Snell was looking directly at me, his face quavering. He had, I recalled, stuck his neck out to let me come here.

I lowered my voice. 'The person who attacked Leo was in this hospital—'

'You assume.'

Don't assume. Classic Garson-roshi teaching. 'I'm on pretty firm ground here. The point is he was wheeled in here and now he's disappeared.'

'It's a big hospital. He could have left through dozens of exits.'

'Or he could still be here. Looking for a second, *easier* shot at Leo.'

'Mr Garson,' the doctor put in, 'is in the recovery room with a team of doctors, nurses, aides, technicians. He will never be alone.'

I'd forgotten the doctor was still here. 'All the easier for the assailant to slip in amidst the flurry and batter him. It'd take seconds. Your staff's watching his vital signs, not for attackers.'

'We do have security here. The sheriff's department—'

John, Snell and I groaned as one. SFPD and the Sheriff of the City and County of San Francisco do not hold each other in high esteem. Some reasons are valid, and some are 49ers–Rams kind of things. John had joined the police force before I started school. There was never a question where our loyalties lay.

The pleasures of speaking one's mind flash strong and fleeting. There are worse things than to hold than your tongue. I took a breath and said, 'Leo was attacked. He's helpless. No one wants to leave him unprotected.'

It ended up that they called security. The sheriff's department agreed to assign a guard. The doctor agreed to make sure he was there. I told the sheriff that Leo was a revered Buddhist teacher – the whole spiel about being part of a large and not-without-influence community in this city – and that my brother was a senior police detective – mumbling over the past tense of the verb – and my sister worked for the *San Francisco Chronicle*. The sheriff's department had been front and center in scandals in the past years. The deputy understood. But none of us appeared happy.

Least of all me. I convinced John to toss Snell a bone and let him deliver me solo to Central Station, the substation which, oddly, covers the northeast corner of the city as opposed to Northern Station in the northwest. If there were an Eastern it'd be in the bay. I figured my chances of waiting for hours at the station to sign my statement were preferable to John delivering me home and devoting hours to sussing out every possible threat of entry in the place.

Half an hour later, Snell deposited me in the waiting room under the eye of the desk sergeant and amidst four college guys who had come to town to patronize the strip clubs on Broadway under the assumption that all strippers are hookers. Two of them wore black hoodies. One looked familiar. The zendo is a block below Broadway. More than once boys have landed in our court-yard after a wide-eyed evening in which they were parted from their pay in just the way the Barbary Coast barkeeps managed it with sailors a hundred and fifty years ago. When their shouts woke him at two or three a.m. Leo would push himself up, cross his legs, then sit zazen and hoped the boys sobered up a bit before driving home. I tried to do likewise. It was one of the reasons the pimp fight had shocked us less than it had John and the reporters.

Now I eyed the one boy in the black hoodie and tried to see his hands. Were they scraped, stained with dried blood? The way he kept his hands in his pockets, we could have been sitting outdoors in Nome. Did he bludgeon Leo, run into traffic, cause an accident, get transported to the hospital, call a car to drive him across town, go to a strip show and almost immediately assault the dancer, patron, bouncer or do something else that landed him in the cop shop? Odds? Not good.

My wait was an hour; statement signing ten minutes. I stepped out onto Vallejo Street at just after two a.m. The detective had offered to find a patrol officer to drive me home, but I'd told him I lived only four blocks away. Even if I'd lived out by the ocean I wouldn't have chosen more open-ended time in the waiting room.

Neither Snell nor this detective had asked why Leo hadn't bounced up to fight off his attacker. Maybe they figured all Buddhists are pacifists. Maybe, in fact, Leo was. Or the answer could have been simpler. It's not easy bouncing to your feet when you're sitting in full lotus, left foot on right thigh, right on left thigh, and wearing a long black robe – all while someone's attacking you.

Columbus Avenue, at close to two on Tuesday morning, was empty. Pacific Avenue was dead still. It wouldn't have surprised me to hear John's car slowly grinding down the street, like a latecomer trying to walk silently across the zendo's creaky floor after everyone was on their cushions facing the wall. Maybe he'd already been by, just not imagining that the cops would leave me waiting an hour and then I'd choose to walk home on the night streets he'd already warned me about . . . repeatedly. Before his retirement he'd been a cloak of warnings; these days, unimpeded by employment, he was heading toward straitjacket-hood.

There was a coziness now to the fog, a sense that perhaps it would shift to rain. The streetlights were blurs on black lines. The courtyard beside the zendo was dark. I peered behind the stone wall just in case – it was easy to miss a man snugged against the wall like a worm in a crevice. I'd done it once or twice. But there was no living thing except the ginkgos in the planters. Reassured, I unlocked the doors and stepped into the hallway Leo had been carried through earlier, and flicked on the light.

At first the place looked utterly normal, as if I was just coming home from a night shoot and I'd be walking softly up the stairs, pausing at the top to listen for the sound of Leo's breathing and slipping into my sleeping bag for a few hours before morning zazen.

Morning zazen! In a little over four hours students, unaware of the attack, would be walking through here to the meditation hall.

Now I saw the entry hall through their eyes. The police had left black powder sprayed on the walls and doorways. The wood plank floor which we swept after every morning zazen, washed on Saturdays and waxed on the full moon weekend was splattered with dirt, leaves, footprints and black scuff marks. Shards of glass sparkled where bare feet would be. And the dokusan room looked like it had been tossed. The two rectangular black zabutans that had lain with the ends almost touching, on which Leo and I sat as he said to me, 'If you meet the Buddha on the road, kill the Buddha,' now lay tossed one atop the other in a corner. Leo's round black *zafu* was gone – had the crime scene unit scooped the cushion up as evidence? The matching cushion I'd sat on was ripped and the white kapok spewed out of the tears. There wasn't as much blood as I'd expected, and I took that as a good sign for Leo. But the ceramic Buddha he had brought back with him from Japan after his years in a monastery there was shattered. I hadn't realized it was hollow.

Hollow! I stared at a pale green shard with gold leaf flecked off at the broken edge. It felt like a sign, an omen.

I shook my head hard, like a dog. We in Zen do not deal in signs and omens and mystical means of manipulating the future. We strive to accept things as they are. 'That's the whole point! Things as they are!' I said aloud in the empty room in the middle of the night.

Then I swept up the pieces and put them in a box. We also don't deal in the kind of miracles it would take to glue it back together. *Kill the Buddha* doesn't mean this, but I wouldn't have been surprised if some ancient roshi had smashed his statue to make his point.

And still 'we clean to clean.' We work in this moment, not for the result. If I'd ever doubted that, I didn't now. I scrubbed every plank from one wall to the other, then started on the next. I didn't think about what had happened or ponder why anyone would attack a decent, sweet man whose first concern was always the dharma. I didn't rebuke myself for not protecting him better (though there were moments I almost slipped into that), nor did I ponder the array of bad outcomes that could await him. I scrubbed.

The dokusan room has no windows. Night is as day. Hours become minutes.

And so, the knock on the courtyard door just about shot me through my skin.

FIVE

I thought – hoped – that knock on the door would be Renzo from Renzo's Caffe, carrying a cup of his superb espresso. A double, because Renzo believed the only reason to drink a single was to remind yourself you should have had a double.

The knock – tap, really – was so slight I wondered if I was half-asleep, half-dreaming it. For the first time since I'd started cleaning the dokusan room I looked at my watch. Over four hours had passed! I pushed myself up. My knees actually creaked. My back felt like something made with an erector set. And, suddenly, I was very, very tired, in the way of one who's been up all night.

And Zen students would be arriving any time now for zazen. I could really use that espresso.

A second tap jolted me into action. I unlocked the door and looked down at the spot where Renzo's been known to leave the little cup.

'Hello.' Lila Suranaman stood so close to the door opening, if there'd been a draft it would have blown her in. She was small – only up to my shoulder and I'm five-six – and South Asian, her English sketchy. Had her English been more extensive she might have said, 'Let me in, now! It's cold out here. Dark. Hurry, I'm scared.'

Behind her, in the courtyard, something moved. A man? A shadow? I blinked a few times but my eyes were too blurry from lack of sleep to see.

And, I realized, there was only fifteen minutes before I needed to clap the clappers to call people to zazen. I took Lila into the kitchen, put on water and showed her the tea selection.

'Thanks.'

'Sure,' I said, and then felt bad about using a word that would only make our colloquialisms more confusing. But, from the look of her, that was the last thing on her mind.

I didn't actually know anything about her, but I'd heard she was a pole dancer in one of the strip clubs on Broadway, a block away. She, of course, didn't speak of it. She appeared for morning zazen two or three times a week, sat dead still in meditation, mouthed sounds in the service as we chanted words she couldn't know and left immediately after the final bell. This morning, as always, a baggy blue sweatshirt hung below her hips over sweatpants of the same color. She had wiped off any make-up and the long hair that probably waved like a flag in the wind as she danced was knotted at the nape of her neck. Her whole presentation screamed *not really a pole dancer*. If she could have melted into the wall, she would have. I wondered what the zendo meant to her, but I couldn't ask.

Ten minutes left now. Hoping for word of Leo, I checked my phone. Of course, there were no voice messages. If anyone from the hospital had called in the middle of the night it would only have been with bad, bad news.

Then, on the path to the least likely, I checked my texts. Six. All from John.

1. Not safe where U are. Come home. Call cab. I'll pay.
2. Drove by. No light. U sleeping?
3. If not, come home. Call. I'll come for U.
4. Be alert. Someone knew where Leo would be. Suspect everyone.
5. Including ur friends. U know how U R about friends.
6. Especially ur friends.

I laughed to myself. John insisted that I could never believe ill of my friends or my family – himself excluded. I always argued, but John was right. And as I watched the sangha members arrive, I certainly did not see them as dangers.

I walked back inside, through the short hallway and pushed open the door to the zendo proper, the meditation room. There is an intimacy about stepping into the room when memories of dark hang like mist and the delicate smell of yesterday's incense clings to the rough surface of the brick walls. The walls of myself are momentarily more porous. Lighting the oil lamps and the candle and seeing the shadows of the altar flowers flicker on the wall pulls me into the silence. I bowed to my seat – this time the one next to the altar – and to the room and sat on my zafu. When everyone was settled I rang the bell, sending out a small, sweet, clear sound, reverberating ever more softly till there was no sound left in the silence.

If we have six people in the zendo, counting Leo and me, in the morning we're doing well. This morning we were doing great. Nine, and that was without Leo. He'd say his absence was stirring up business.

Slowly the dark lifted and the shaded forms sitting cross-legged on black cushions hardened into distinctness. Four of the people I knew. Five strangers. Police? Reporters? Coincidence? Or was one of them the assailant? A gray-haired woman sat dead still. A blonde was doing her best. And a wiry woman with a puff of brown wiry curls alternated between stillness and jerking. One of the two new men shifted his legs, settled in and shifted again in ever more rapid progression. An older man took the stoic route, but he looked miserable.

Halfway through the sitting period the hallway door opened. A body leaned in and hesitated. Snell! I could read his orders in his widened eyes, in those thick shoulders that hunched hopefully back toward the hallway. *Go get her. Watch what she does. Bring her back in.* I thought for an instant that he'd trot right in, plant himself in front of me and start spewing orders. But I was wrong. Way wrong.

He eyed the zafus with an expression of horror, as if lowering himself onto one of those small round cushions would be akin to balancing on one foot. Then he spotted the folding chairs we keep along the wall and sat on one of them. I thought he'd squirm and he did. Folding chairs are folding chairs, after all. But he didn't scratch, shift his jacket, look around or do any extraneous thing. He sat as still as he could, and rose tremendously in my opinion.

Without moving her head, Lila took him in, figured he was a cop, I was sure, and continued to sit.

At the end of the period, when I rang the bell, I'd almost forgotten about Snell. As the seven others stood, straightened their knees and their zabutans and re-puffed their cushions, I said, 'This service is dedicated to the well-being of Garson-roshi who—'

Gasps came from both sides of the zendo. The roshi in need of healing? Snell's eyes shot back and forth, noting, I was sure, who was surprised and, more to the point, who was not. The reactions were from the regulars. The two new men seemed dazed. The gray-haired woman just looked puzzled. But Lila let out a gasp.

Snell eyed me and coughed. Loud. He put his finger across his lips.

'—is in the hospital.'

Every morning after zazen we chant the Heart Sutra, the heart of the very long sutra that puts into words that which cannot be described in words. In a well-being ceremony we do the same thing, add a *dharani* – short section of a sutra – and dedicate the merit of the chanting to the sick person. Is there merit in chanting? I don't know. Does the effect of the chanting float beyond the walls of this room, beyond influencing what we do on the other side of the zendo doors? I don't know. But today, when our voices – Snell's included – raggedly chanted the Heart Sutra: *Form is no different from emptiness, emptiness no different from form,* that comfort was enough.

Then Snell said to the group, 'I'm Officer Snell. I need a moment of your time before you leave.'

And I added, 'Please leave the zendo before you speak to the officer.'

Seven faces showed displeasure. It was already 7:50 a.m. *Tempus fugit* in the work world. And in the world of the laid back, no one wants to talk to a cop before breakfast. People hurried to the hall to ask Snell for a pass.

I waited till they left, trimmed the candle, sifted the ash and straightened the altar for the evening sitting. I aligned the zabutans.

Lila was standing in a corner, full into it, and so unobtrusive I almost overlooked her. It was more than her dark hair and dark garb that camouflaged her – there was something about her carriage, the forward curve of her shoulders and her drooped head, as if she had been trained or had learned to melt into shadows. Like a child in a world where beauty was a curse.

But she couldn't stay in here. I opened the door, motioned her out and said to Snell, 'Lila is one of our regular members, but English is difficult for her.' So basically: lay off her.

Then I watched as she bowed to him the way she would to the Buddha and offered, the way she would when presenting the Buddha flowers or incense, a shy just-for-him smile.

She wasn't going to need my help with him!

I shut the door and pressed my ear against the crack.

SIX

ere's what I learned, ear to door: Snell had dismissed the first of the two male strangers and was interviewing the second, 'Mr Something-like-Golf Cart,' who was complaining loud enough for me to stand up straight and not near the door. 'You let him go. He's a stringer. He's already peddling his story to every outlet in town, including *my* editor. While I'm standing around here telling you, again, that I've never been in this place before, I don't know these people. I'm here because I get up before dawn to check the police beat. I caught a break on this Buddhist priest attack deal. So I could break this story, that, now, *he's* going to break if I don't get out of here.'

Snell's voice barely carried, his words not at all. What came through loud and strong was his tempo. Slow lane. Like the driver who's been beeped at just lifting his foot off the gas. I could almost see Snell grinning in the rearview mirror.

'No! Nothing! *Officer!* What do you expect me to have seen? I was sitting on the floor, with my nose three inches from the wall and my knees so jammed I was lucky the cartilage didn't go shooting across the room.'

So he was the squirmer I'd noted in the zendo – short and thin, hips so tight his knees were nearly in his armpits. I'd thought of quietly suggesting a higher cushion to ease those knees. Too late now. Chances of seeing Mr Golf Cart-or-whatever again here were equal to meeting the Buddha on the road.

It annoyed me, though, how quickly Leo had become a commodity. To Golf Cart, to Snell, to the stringer racing out for his big break. As if Leo, my teacher, my friend, had desiccated into a few key strokes.

It was 8:00 a.m. Surely there should be some word on Leo. Had he passed a restful night? Was he markedly improving, not seeing double, his headache almost gone, not nauseous? Minimally, the guard was still by his bed and he was safe? I stepped out into the hall then slipped into the kitchen and checked my phone. Zip. Not even a finger-wagging text from John, much less a forwarded update. Maybe my brother was finally sleeping. But Leo . . . As soon as Snell cleared out of here I'd make tracks for the hospital. The sheriff was guarding him, right? He'd be fine, right?

Snell was verbally hanging onto Tully Lennox, a thirty-ish morning zazen regular for the last couple months. Tully was pulling his jacket tighter around his beanpole body and listing toward the door. In a minute he'd be stretching fabric trying to pull free.

'. . . So you were in that interview room with him right before the attack.'

'Not *right* before.'

'Within the hour, correct, Mr Lennox?'

'Honestly, I didn't see anyone, Officer. Like I said—' Tully was anxious. He was frustrated. He looked like his tightly curled blond hair was about to uncork off his head.

'You walked to the corner. Who'd you see there?'

'No one. I was looking for my car.'

'Are you certain, Mr Lennox? Think carefully.'

Tully was uneasy at the best of times and now he looked like he was envisioning solitary confinement. I wanted to save him but I knew better, so I slipped by into the courtyard. The zazen regulars who had gasped at the news of Leo were waiting, hoping I would answer questions for which I had no answers.

With its high gray stone wall, potted plants and low stone fence, the courtyard looks like Italy. On mornings like this it feels like Norway. Renzo had set up a table of Renzo's Caffe coffee and pastries. I looked around for him, our big friendly bear of a neighbor. Normally he'd be here, greeting morning sitters like this was his place. The stiff, slightly bitter aroma of his very serious coffee would mix with the whiffs of almond paste or pistachio, orange, lemon or perhaps cherry in the pastry of the day. It did now, but somehow, without him here to offer it, the courtyard seemed all the colder. Even non-coffee drinkers were holding cups for warmth. In a few hours the fog might roll back over the Pacific and the sun sparkle like someone had thrown the switch. Or ambivalent February could switch back to winter rain.

'I can't believe it,' a blonde woman, Caroline, was saying as Tully hurried over, his face blinking between frazzle and relief, and grabbed a pastry, knocked over a coffee cup and caught everyone in the swirl of removing the innocent stain from the stones. A woman I hadn't seen before this morning's sitting – the wiry puff of hair woman – grabbed a napkin, bent from the waist and started mopping. The squirmer stood behind her, now suddenly still, watching us all. Observing, stuffing Renzo's pastries in his mouth and managing to demand of Tully, 'What'd he want? The cop?'

Tully pushed himself up. 'Wanted to know what happened yesterday when I had dokusan. I go, "Nothing." But he's not having that, you know? He asks again, like he's trying to make fire with a flint – you know, like if he keeps striking I'll flame him out something.'

'So nothing?' Caroline prompted.

'No, I wasn't looking, I had . . . things . . . on my mind. Really, there could have been a platypus lying against the wall and I wouldn't have noticed. I gotta . . . go.' He looked at me. 'Can I see Leo? Call him?'

'I'll let you know.'

Behind Tully, the squirmer pulled a pad out of a pocket of his dark tweed jacket and moved up next to the mopper. She edged away.

I said, 'I'm going to go back to the hospital.'

'Will you let us know—'

'Of course. Give me your numbers.'

They say people expose themselves in times of stress. Maybe. Maybe not. But here they all gave their snapshots. Caroline – ever organized – pulled out a pad, wrote, tore off the sheet and passed it to Tully. He pulled at his long, prominent chin. He had intermittent aspirations of a beard. He'd let his stubble grow, sometimes for a few days, sometimes a couple of weeks before annoyance, frustration or a girlfriend's ultimatums perhaps brought him to blade. The beard came and went, but the chin rubbing remained. He gave his chin a last pull before accepting the pen and paper and excavating his memory for the number. The squirmer grabbed and pressed so hard the pen ripped the paper. And the gray-haired woman held the pad and said to me,

'This is my first time here. I heard Garson-roshi speak in Berkeley. Is this OK? I don't want to—'

'It's fine, really,' I said.

The mopper was just about bouncing. She'd almost grabbed the paper twice. I didn't know her either but she wasn't asking permission. 'You're Darcy?' She handed me the paper as if it was a missive between the two of us and glanced behind her as if to be sure no one was near.

'Yes.'

'Aurelia Abernathy. Aurelia Anne. My brothers are Adam and Alexander. You know, like we're a cute collection. It's a whole A-full household. Too much information?' She laughed. 'Sorry. I know this is a bad, bad time. I mean, I know Leo. What I mean is I knew him before, you know? I didn't know about this, the attack though. I'm stunned. Leo, wow, he's the last person, right? Sorry.'

I nodded. This was one woman with whom I wasn't going to have to worry about what to say. In a subdued post-meditation group she was like the dandelion in the lawn that Dad would aim the mower over and find it had popped up behind him. She was an odd combination of thin and muscular, of direct and edgy. Her hair was curlier than mine, but brown and short, the kind of hair you don't even have to run your fingers through, like ground cover on the head. She shifted from foot to foot as if all that sitting so still in the zendo had sucked out all her ballast and now she was bobbing on the water. I said, 'You know Leo from . . .?'

'Japan.'

'Really?' Despite Leo and I living across the hall from each other, my being his assistant, him being my teacher, he kept the gate to his past closed. Partly out of respect and partly from fear of offending, hurting and stepping onto too soft ground, I stayed on the outside. That's not to say I wasn't curious. Au contraire. 'In the monastery?' Safe guess, that.

'Yes. He was much more serious – established, if that's the term. I wasn't there long.'

'Just passing through?'

'You could say that.'

'School trip?' She looked young and haggard at the same time, like she'd just finished high-school exams and done all-nighters for the lot of them. But even if she'd been in high school when she and Leo were in Japan, how many years ago could that have been? Looks can be deceiving. Billions of dollars support that! Even factoring in face goo, grin-and-grimace exercises and just good luck, she couldn't have been much over thirty now.

'Sort of. But listen, this is the wrong time. Since I've got you, you know . . . I just got here. You're a stuntwoman, right?'

'Stunt double, yes.'

'Do you think I can break in?'

'What?' *What!*

'Oh, sorry, this was so stupid of me. Of course, you've got too much on your mind right now. Forget I asked. I'll catch you later, when things are calmer. When Leo's back. When do you think that'll be? I mean, I know hospitals toss you out as soon as you can remember your name. My sister-in-law had a baby and was home the next day.'

I offered an all-inclusive, 'Thanks.' Then thought to add, 'Where can I reach you, Aurelia?' I'd be giving Leo a blow-by-blow account of this scene and he might want to know. Though, if he was wise, he wouldn't.

But I'd never once seen him sidestep a student or anyone else to avoid being chattered at. He listened to whoever came, regardless of all the very good reasons – time, manners, personal hygiene – that argued against it. When I'd challenge him, he'd quote the opening lines of Third Patriarch's Xin Xin Ming:

> *The Great Way is not difficult,*
> *it only excludes picking and choosing.*

Aurelia wrote down her cell number and fluttered off, sucking all the energy out of the courtyard with her and leaving it icier than before. If the fog was going to lift today, it was giving no warning. Tully was gone, Caroline on her way out and the strangers nowhere in sight now. I trudged down the half block to Renzo's and the promise of another espresso and comfort.

When I'd first seen Renzo in a rumpled jacket, squirming on a zafu in the dawn zendo, I'd assumed he was a plump, gray-curled derelict who'd found a quiet place to get warm. It hadn't occurred to me that the pastry baker who kept an eye on the block from his tiny cafe on the corner would be checking out his new neighbors' operation. Even less would I have imagined that he would fold our morning zazen into his daily schedule, unlock the zendo if neither of us was there and have espresso waiting afterward. He was so regular that I could have sworn I smelled that coffee brewing half a block away every morning when I rang the final bell.

Renzo had grown up in this part of the city. He was not only a native San Franciscan, as I myself was, but a much-esteemed fourth generation. And all four of his generations had lived their lives within half a mile of this spot. He was on first-name terms with all established shopkeepers, restaurateurs, the managers of the strip clubs that had lined Broadway long enough to be considered for city landmark status. If you'd lived here more than a couple years, Renzo knew you. He kept contact with his friends from high school, from his days at San Francisco State. He had relatives in every part of the city, every municipal agency, in city hall and on both sides of the law. There was nothing Renzo couldn't find out. In Zen there is a saying: *Not knowing is the most perfect.* For Renzo, not knowing was an insult. This was his city and he gathered its facts and whispers with a collector's passion.

As soon as I opened the door into the white-on-white little cafe with its three empty round tables, I could tell he had news. Bad news. Even the smell of sweet, warm pastry couldn't soften that. Now I realized why he hadn't been in the courtyard. He'd been on the phone.

I'd have been shocked if he hadn't heard about Leo's attack. He had a female relative – niece, cousin? – who worked at SF General. A nurse, I thought. He probably had her horse's-mouthing from Leo's doctors, nurses and the guard at the door.

An espresso and a morning bun were waiting at the table nearest the counter. I sat and picked up the bun.

Before I could speak, Renzo said, 'Leo's gone.'

I gasped. The pastry fell to the table, rolled to the edge and over onto the floor. 'Leo's dead?'

'No, no! He's just not in the hospital any more.'

'How could he be gone? What about the guard?'

'No guard.'

'Snell assured me there would be a guard on his door.'

'He ordered one. Shift ended. No replacement.'

'And Leo? Did they move him? Transfer him? Lose him?' SF General had lost a patient for weeks a year or so ago. If Leo got separated from his chart or ID bracelet . . . If he was comatose, or just out of it, he could be anywhere. Getting no treatment. Or worse, getting someone else's meds.

'What about his attacker?'

Renzo shook his head. He loved Leo; he hated not knowing. It was the worst combination for him.

I stared at my cup. I had to do something, pronto. My mind went to green screen. All roads led to detour. Go to the hospital? And do what? Troll floor after floor, sticking my head into each room? Startle the sick? Peek under the sheets of the not-quite-visible? Try to vanish when I smacked into a doctor making rounds? And when I finished, should I start over again because they could have moved him in that time? I sipped. Even espresso didn't help. It just let me see more clearly that I didn't know what to do.

Renzo offered a fresh morning bun.

I nodded and nibbled. 'Your niece or cousin—'

'Cousin's daughter-in-law. Loretta, the doctor.'

'What did she suggest? Suppose it was her patient who disappeared?' I almost said: *Did you ask her that?*

But of course he had. For Renzo, leaving a question unasked was akin to leaving dough unbaked. 'She'd have reviewed the chart, called in the nursing sup., phoned the nurses at home, the ones who'd gone off shift. And then' – his shoulders straightened just a bit, and his chest puffed like a tiny bird taking its first proud breath – 'she'd do the same with the LVN's, the assistants and the cleaning staff.'

Really? Or did she just know how to deal with Renzo? 'Can she do that for Leo?'

It was a moment before he said, in a small voice, 'No.'

'Of course not. I shouldn't have asked.' I'd felt overwhelmed before. Loretta had merely confirmed my fears. Needle in a haystack. Grain on a beach. Even if I called everyone I knew . . .

But I couldn't just do nothing. I had to find him. 'I'm going to have to suck it up,' I said, 'and call everyone I can trust.'

'How're you going to make that evaluation? How're you going to finger the one who could go bad? The villain who stabbed Leo walked into the building, right? No one said, "Man, you are one suspicious-looking dude."'

I nodded. Sipped.

'The borderlines who come to sit zazen; the ones you can't vouch for, not when we're talking life or death – how're you going to keep them from finding out they fell off the bad side of that fence of yours?'

'Yeah,' I said, letting that single word substitute for the answer, which I did not have. 'I'll go with blood, I guess. My brothers and Gracie.'

Renzo grinned. 'Detective John Lott, Attorney Gary Lott, Doctor Grace Lott, all with years of experience giving orders. Expecting to snap-to cooperation. Tell me, Darcy, do you figure you'd be in charge of this operation?'

I had. A minute earlier. 'I can't just wait and see. Leo could be lying in a corner in the hospital behind the laundry wagon. Or in an empty room with the guy with a billy club. I can't— Did you ask Loretta about his prognosis?'

Renzo gave his 'of course' move. It must have been automatic by now. 'That's the good news. The concussion's serious, but there's no sign of brain damage.'

Brain damage! That horrifying thought hadn't even entered my mind!

'So, you see it's not as bad as maybe you thought. They'd've been discharging him in a day or two anyway.'

That from Loretta's interpolation from the words on his chart, written how long ago? Right after the surgery? When he was in recovery? How long before he disappeared? How accurate?

Renzo said something but I couldn't hear him over the clatter of a car clanking around the corner from Columbus Avenue. If it had been a scrap metal truck it couldn't have managed a greater rattle. 'What the—'

Our street, Pacific Avenue, is one way. The *other* way.

'Tourist,' Renzo muttered, without scorn. Renzo adored tourists, loved serving them real San Francisco coffee in a real San

Francisco cafe. He just about preened when they asked him questions about his city.

The rattle was slowing like a tambourine in a tired hand. And then it gave a final shake and stopped.

In front of the zendo.

SEVEN

The car, an old white BMW, one of the ones with big windows all around, had rattled to a halt by the curb next to the courtyard. I could smell its exhaust inside the cafe. The driver, a burly guy in a faded blue zip jacket and jeans that had seen cleaner days – I could tell that from this distance – pushed himself out from behind the wheel and pulled open the rear driver's-side door.

For a moment he stood leaning in toward the back seat, as if unsure what to do. He had the look of a guy who was unsure a lot.

I leaned closer to the cafe window just as a foot stuck out toward him from the back seat. Had it been moving fast, it would have hit his knee and sent him flying across the sidewalk. Or worse. But it just hung there, like rubber.

A bare foot.

Extending out of a black robe.

I shot out the cafe door and down the street, slid in front of the driver and stared into the car. 'Omigod! Leo!'

Leo lay crumpled against the far window. He looked just like he had on the dokusan room floor – fragile, shaky and gray, his bare feet poking out of his black robe. He looked like he was about to go sweaty all over the black leather seat. His face was ashen, punctuated by big blotches of red-purple. He looked like death not bothering to warm over.

I reached for his hand, just to touch him. It was clammy. 'Let me help you stretch out. We'll get an ambulance—'

'No,' he rasped. How long had it been since he'd even had water?

'I'll ride back to the hospital with you. I won't let you out of my sight.'

'No.'

'You have to—'

'No!'

'But—'

He struggled to draw in a breath. 'Inside.' His voice was barely audible but there was no arguing with him.

Renzo opened the other door and I maneuvered Leo out. I probably could have carried him myself if I'd had to. Stronger-than-she-looks is a baseline necessity in my line of work. But Renzo and I clasped hands and made a seat of sorts, then pushed close enough for Leo to lean against our shoulders. He was hanging onto our arms like they were the chains of a swing, our clasped hands a seat he might go sailing off at any moment. But his grasp was so weak it barely compressed my skin.

It wasn't till we had edged awkwardly up the stairs and lowered him onto the futon in his room that it struck me he had never even protested or tried to stand up.

While Renzo helped him out of his clothes, I stepped into the hall where the driver stood, looking every bit as nonplussed as he had on the sidewalk. His back was against the bathroom door. Small as this hallway was, it had to be against one of the doors – mine, Leo's, bathroom or closet – that or teetering at the top of the stairs. He was fingering the pull tab on his jacket zipper. The slider was only connected to one side and it shot up and down fast and uselessly. He had that smell Mom called 'Eau de Haight.' Dust and sweat, marinated, all undiluted by laundering, found in the unattached male. His ensemble was spiced with the scent of car oil, as if he'd been under the hood and wiped his hands on, of course, his jeans.

'Are you a cab driver?' His vehicle had no sign, but there are a number of steps between private vehicle and officially registered and medallion-paid taxis in San Francisco.

'No.'

'Then how did you—'

'He called me.'

'From the hospital?'

'I guess.'

Was I going too fast here? 'Where did you pick him up?'

'On a bench by the hospital.'

'He was sitting upright on a bench? He was in that good a shape half an hour ago?'

'Must've taken all his strength. I got him in the car. He just, like, melted. Like he was an old man. I'll tell you I was worried. I told him, "You need to turn around and go right in there. The hospital, I mean." We were right there and all. But he kept saying no. He said to bring him here.'

Inadequately suppressed groans and whispered 'Sorry's' came in spurts from behind Leo's closed doors. I so wanted to help, but of course I couldn't. The room was already crowded with the two of them in there.

The not-cab driver seemed just to be waiting.

'Thanks. Really.' I glanced into my room across the hall, looking for my wallet. 'Let me pay you.'

'No! No, I'm glad to— If there's anything . . .'

'Sure.'

Surprisingly, he extracted a business card.

Hudson Poulsson
Man of all Trades

No phone number. 'How is it you know Leo?'

'Garson-roshi? He did me a big favor once. I . . . I gotta go before the meter maid . . . you know?'

This from a guy who parked the wrong way on a one-way street. If traffic cops started writing tickets for his vehicular sins, it would be cheaper for Hudson Poulsson to give them his car. 'Thanks, Hudson. Keep in touch, OK? Write down your number.'

'Yeah,' he said, and turned toward the stairs.

But he didn't start down them. He stood. Indecision really was his natural state.

As he was hanging around, I said, 'Hudson, what was it Leo did for you?' Either he'd answer or leave. With luck, both.

'He, uh, wrote to me when I couldn't get out.'

Out of the house? Of bed? In a monastery far in the mountains or deep in the desert? Or a lock-up, criminal or mental? Wherever he'd been he'd sure shown up pronto when Leo needed him. 'Thanks,' I said again, 'it's not a small thing to have a friend you can count on.'

But I did wonder why had Leo thought of him? Why of all his friends, students and all the cabs and for-hire cars was Hudson Poulsson the one Leo called? It wasn't like Leo had a wallet with him. Was Poulsson the one whose phone number he knew by heart?

'If I can do anything, just ask,' Poulsson said. And then he clattered down the stairs, the human reflection of his vehicle, leaving me facing the tsunami of problems requiring decisions, none of which I'd have sufficient knowledge to handle. First was getting a doctor in here.

I called my sister, Gracie. She'd lay out to Leo, in six syllable words, just how dire his situation was, how much he needed to stay in bed, and follow the directions of the practicing MD she, the epidemiologist, would find for him.

Her phone went to voicemail. I dialed again . . . and got voicemail again. 'This is Doctor Grace Lott. I will be unavailable until Monday. If this is an emergency, call nine-one-one. If you need immediate access to data, and it absolutely can't wait till Monday, call my assistant, Carmela Capistrano at . . .' Paper rustling sounds scraped the line. It was so like Gracie not to have the number handy.

But it *was* on my phone. I called Carmela. 'How can I reach Gracie?' I asked after ritual greetings.

'Leave her a message. She's at a conference. In Vegas.'

'I just tried. Got her voicemail. It sent me to you.'

'OK, OK.' She gave a harrumphy sigh. I'd heard that a lot from Carmela. If you had an epidemiological crisis, Gracie was the best – smart, tireless, totally focused. Which meant she was totally unfocused on everything else. Which also meant Carmela sighed a lot. 'I'll tell her when she checks in.'

'When will that be?'

'Oh, I don't know.'

'What's the subject of the conference?'

'MERS, I think. But I could be wrong. She was deciding between a couple of different ones.'

Really? Topics so equally appealing Gracie couldn't make up her mind till the last minute? But I didn't have time to worry about that now. 'Her hotel?'

'Well, it depends on her choice.'

'Carmela! Never mind. Just, please, ask her to call me. It's serious.'

'Can I tell her what it's about?'

'Just say it's important. Really important.'

Now what? I'd been counting on Gracie to whip over, eyeball Leo and pronounce a verdict. She was my only medical resource and happy to be so. I couldn't—

The door opened. Renzo emerged, his normally competent, mayor-of-the-block persona replaced by frazzle. His jacket was askew – even his wavy gray hair poked up as if he'd been pulling his fingers through it. I was afraid to ask about Leo.

'See for yourself,' he said.

EIGHT

There is no living room or even common space upstairs above the zendo. Leo's room was where we talked. He'd sit on his futon and I'd lean against the far wall bemoaning the Giants' summer slump, eating pizza from the box that filled the space between us, talking about what friends talk about. California threatening to end its tax break to the movie industry? I'd grumbled about it there. Dearth of stunt gigs, my favorite second unit director moving to Toronto, new animation making inroads into the shrinking stunt world? Most recently I'd tried for equanimity when a movie company with a hot-shot second unit director set up on the top of Lombard and didn't call me for stunts on the famous 'crookedest street.' We'd talk about— Me! We'd talk about my career, my family, me!

We did not, I suddenly realized, ever discuss Leo's family, his life before he became the abbot of a monastery in the woods hours north of the city or his lovers. Marriages? I'd had a brief one. Him? No. Zen, he'd said, was too demanding a mistress. We live and die in every moment. He wasn't interested in resurrecting.

He would have a pot of tea already steeped on a tray beside his futon, his small cup partially filled and another waiting for me, a sign of his willingness to answer my questions. My dharma questions.

Rarely, but sometimes, the teapot would be empty and he'd ask me to go through the process of rinsing it out, heating the water, warming the pot, emptying that water and pouring the boiled water onto the leaves, the ritual being not merely for the drink, but the attention it demanded. More than once, by the time I'd made the tea, the answer to my dilemma had steeped through the waltz of the ritual.

Tea had been such a constant in here, the room held its earthy, pungent scent.

Renzo had left, but the door to Leo's room was still shut. I knocked and when I heard Leo's voice, pushed open the door.

What hit me right off was the smell of sick. Remnants of nausea, of sweat, blotches of dried blood. Leo lay with his eyes swollen almost closed, purple bruises like goggles around them. His ear was bloated, the skin on that vertical channel ripped. It looked like someone had dumped scalding water on his shaved scalp. His hands, on the outside of the covers, quivered.

In my memory of the attack he'd only been struck once. Not again and again like this. 'Oh, Leo!'

He tried for a smile. Normally his features seemed too big for his head, but now they fit right in, his bulb of a nose like a pale bud underneath the blossoming bouquet of his face. 'I know what you're thinking,' he said. 'But I'm not going back to the hospital.'

'Big surprise.'

Now he did manage a shadow of a smile.

'Nevertheless, Leo, you can't just lie here and hope. We Zen types don't deal in miracles.'

'Still, not going.'

Still, big surprise. 'I left a message for Gracie, but she's off in Vegas and who knows when she'll check in? Do you have a doctor?'

I was so sure he'd say 'No' that I was deciding whether to get Renzo looking for one, or Mom, when he stopped me mid-thought. 'Call Nezer Deutsch. His number's in my book.'

'Nezer?'

'Ebenezer . . . He's a twin. His brother's called Ben.'

'Hard luck.'

'Life as it is.' One of the Zen aphorisms. We look at life as it is, rather than deluding ourselves with dreams of better nicknames, or complaints about the twin who got there first.

His eyes fluttered shut. I wanted to leave him to sleep, but I said, 'Leo, someone tried to kill you. That person was carried into the hospital minutes after you arrived. He was in the hospital when you were. Did he come after you there?'

His throat tightened as if he was willing the muscles to support sound. 'No.'

'When he burst past me to attack you, in the dokusan room, you saw him, right? Do you know him?'

'I remember . . . someone . . . big hurry. Bent over . . . and . . . No more.'

Concussion! Of course he didn't remember. *Contre-coups.*
Still, I said, 'You must have looked up.'

'Yes, I saw . . . dark.'

The damned hoodie.

His hand started moving, feeling around on the blanket. 'My
kotsu? Where is my kotsu?'

'I don't know.'

'Oh.' It was all he said. Not even a sigh with the sound. His
teacher had given it to him. It was a symbol not only of his own
worthiness as a teacher, but also their bond. I wanted to say the
police were on the hunt, but they probably weren't. If the assailant
had had it in the hospital it could be under any table, bed or pile.
If he'd tossed it before . . . 'We'll scour the neighborhood.'

'Life as it is.'

Before I could reply, the slit of his eyes disappeared. This time
they did not open.

I eased up to standing, found his address book and called
Nezer Deutsch. I got him, not his service. Deutsch wasn't a-bubble
with enthusiasm, but I'd already been through Gracie vanishing
into Las Vegas and I wasn't about to cut this doctor slack. 'Leo
asked specifically for you,' I said. 'How soon can you be here?
Someone's already attacked him. I don't want to be leaving the
outside door open forever.' He hemmed, and I added, 'If anything
happens to Leo it'll be on your head.'

He caved. 'Within the hour.'

Then I pulled my sleeping bag into the hall, lay down by Leo's
door and waited. I listened while he breathed, on edge for any
gasp or cough, for any sign his face wasn't giving me.

If I hadn't fallen asleep I might have conjured a picture of Leo's
chosen physician. I might have known if he arrived within the
hour. But sleep turned out to have been foremost for both Leo
and me. I make it a point never to tot up the inadequate number
of sacked-out minutes I've had the previous night. I just charge
on into the coming day.

Whatever, I was zonked. When shoe leather smacked the
wooden stairs it took me almost the entire flight to realize what
that noise was. And the first thing I saw of Nezer Deutsch was
his tan sock.

'Leo?'

'You are?' I snapped, matching his testy tone. I wriggled warp speed out of my bag and shoved myself up to standing.

'Doctor Deutsch.'

'He's in his room.' I knocked.

A pale sound came from inside. I opened the door and peered around.

Leo looked just as I'd left him, as if he hadn't moved at all, hadn't had the strength to. His face was the same purple on gray, but his hands weren't quivering and his skin wasn't as sweaty. I took that as a ridiculously good sign.

In fact, Dr Deutsch looked not much better – like an intern who'd been on duty for the last ninety-six hours. Older, though – maybe mid-thirties. His too-thin body hung on a frame which was meant to be meaty. His straight brown hair screamed, *Cut at a kid's barber*. And he had a wary look that's the last thing you want in the person assessing you for life or death. I had intended to give Leo some privacy with his physician. Now I motioned to Deutsch to follow me in.

Leo's eyes eased shut. The doctor knelt, shifting the brown blanket Leo had so proudly acquired from a catalog sporting Swedish army blankets for twenty dollars. I'd wondered more than once just which war or wars it had been through. Knees on wood, Deutsch assessed Leo, like a surgeon triple-checking before the first cut. He inhaled, closed his eyes and picked up Leo's wrist – in that order.

Then, as if he'd burst through a wall, he opened his eyes and gently palpated Leo's forehead, fingered the sides of his neck, pulled back the blanket, lifted Leo's white T-shirt, listened to his heart, felt his flesh.

The floor was hard against my own knees but I didn't dare move. The air seemed clammy from all our exhalations. There was no incense. If I'm here making tea, Leo always burns incense. He'll be OK, I told myself. After all, the doctor's not panicked.

'I'm going to check your abdomen,' the doctor said to Leo.

I was on the verge of demanding why when it struck me that he was really asking Leo if he wanted to be laid out bare in front of me.

'I can wait outside the door.' *In earshot.*

'Fine. You—'

'Go downstairs. Make us tea.' Leo's eyes remained closed but his voice was surprisingly firm. It did not invite questions.

'OK. Bang on the floor if you need me.' I pushed up gratefully and stiff-legged it down the stairs.

We have a makeshift kitchen behind the staircase. At some point in its history the building had been the kind of restaurant that had a cloakroom. It had to have had a serious kitchen, too, but there's no trace of that now. What we inherited was a one-person space that accommodates a sink, a refrigerator under a counter that I could span with my forearm, a narrow cabinet and one of those slits of glass that says, 'Code insists we put in a window. Take this!' There's no place to store the kettle but that doesn't matter because it's always on one of the two electric burners that we consider a stove.

The process of making tea cannot be rushed. Leo might as easily have told me to give him ten minutes' privacy. This was hardly a tea ceremony but I approached it with the same focus, giving my full attention to the pouring of the water, the lifting of the black iron pot, the spooning of the flaky leaves. I did not indulge the 'what ifs' that were clawing at the roots of my hair. I listened to the burble of water in the pan. I listened to my own breath. As the Zen teachings say, I did the next thing.

When I carried the tray upstairs, the doctor was standing in Leo's doorway.

Ignoring his eagerness to leave, I herded him back in, knelt, placed the tray on the floor beside Leo, rocked back on my heels and stood.

'How is he?'

'Not terminal,' Leo said, preemptively silencing Deutsch.

'What instructions—'

Deutsch held out a paper. 'Here.'

'Do you—'

A phone rang. My phone. I'd forgotten it was in my pocket. I shrugged a sorry, blocked the door lest the man tried to escape and checked the display, hoping this was the moment Gracie had chosen to call back. Hoping she could give me advice about Leo and the lowdown on Deutsch.

'Who is it?' Leo asked.

'My agent. I'll call—'

'No. Take it.'

I hesitated but there was no *if* in his voice. Tight as the movie market was in San Francisco, which he'd heard about from me just yesterday, he didn't want to be responsible for me missing a gig. I nodded, stepped into my room and heard the golden words: big gag set-up, action movie, actress asked for you. The crookedest street gag! 'But . . .' An eternity passed before my agent's new assistant, Mel, said, 'It's Dainen Beretski.'

'Wow! Didn't he do *Surreptitious*? With that great triple transfer? Bike to plane to raft?'

'Uh huh.'

'But . . .?' *Spit it out, man!*

'I've heard . . . well, you're a seasoned pro. Just be careful.'

'Of my neck or my ass?'

'Both, honeybun. If you don't have a good ass, your neck's not going to matter.'

'Can you be more specific?'

'Nothing concrete; I'm just shooting the shit with you.'

I could have pushed him, but I gave up. No matter what he said I wasn't about to turn down this gig. Not in a million years! I wanted to jump, to shout, to race in and grab Leo by the shoulders and dance around the room. A gig! Not only a gig, but one on a picture with a high-powered, innovative, attention-getting hot-shot second unit director! Not even the cut-rate pay but the full SAG rate. Yesterday I was sure I'd have to give up my career or my place here with Leo. Yesterday my career was in the past. Now I was headed to the fast lane!

Leo was back home, he'd be OK. I had a job. My problems were over! I said into the phone, 'What time?'

'Be there at five.'

'At night?'

'Before dawn.'

I grabbed a pad, wrote down names and numbers, then clicked off.

And in that time Dr Nezer Deutsch had moved his gaunt and oppugnant self down the stairs and was gone. Leo lay with the covers over his chin and his eyes shut, breathing like he could be asleep in two seconds.

I hated to keep him awake. 'What did he say, the doctor?'

'Fine,' he muttered. 'I'll be fine.'

'In the meantime? Specifically?'

'Rest.'

'Leo!'

'Darcy!'

Mocking me – a good sign.

I'd seen concussions, even had one or two. But they'd been mild and all I remembered in the way of treatment was the medic on the set waking me up when I was desperate to sleep. 'Will he be checking on you tomorrow?' I asked Leo.

'Sure. I'll be fine.'

'You bet.'

The rest of the day I devoted to sleep, waking, waking an ungrateful Leo, making soup, hunting down what I could about the movie company, Dainen Beretski, the second unit director and the script. The high point of adventure was a walk to Columbus and back on the other side of the street, eyes scanning the ground for Leo's kotsu, which I did not expect to find and, indeed, did not find.

By the next morning, I felt normal. Or what passes for normal when dawn is just a distant hope.

'I hate to wake you, Leo.'

'What time is it?' He looked, of course, groggy, but he'd regained some color.

'Twenty after four.'

'You better get going!'

He remembered my five o'clock call! Good sign. He really was getting better. 'Let me check your bruises.'

'They're fine. Just ugly.'

'Still, I—'

'Doctor Darcy? Nezer'll be here.'

'When?'

'Before work.'

'Still—'

'I'm fine.'

I stared pointedly at the wounds and laughed. And in a moment he smiled, sort of. 'I'm adequate,' he said.

'I'll be the judge of that. I'm not leaving till I see you stand up.'

He grunted, then nodded toward the bathroom. I'd helped him there twice in the evening and once a couple hours ago, and had been encouraged that he was steady enough to handle the trips. 'Prospect of the bedpan,' he'd said, 'makes miracles.'

'I'll be back by the end of zazen,' I said.

'I'll be fine by myself. Go!'

So, I went. Hesitantly, uneasily, and with guilt for desperately wanting to be out and on the set.

Leo's a grown man; he's survived this long, he can take care of himself, I told myself. Then insisted, It's only a concussion. I've had worse.

The outer door was locked. The doctor was coming. In less than two hours Renzo would check on him before he hit the clappers for morning zazen. What could happen in two hours?

NINE

Wind smacked my hair in my face. Big-time wind.

San Francisco is built on seven major hills, though it has forty-nine named hills. I was standing atop Russian Hill, so called after a long-gone cemetery for nineteenth-century Russian sailors. But what it's famed for is the 'crookedest street in the world' – Lombard, the block between Hyde and Leavenworth. It's the lemon to lemonade of street reconfiguration. Transformed from a death-on-brakes descent to eight colorfully landscaped switchbacks. Steering down it is akin to doing a square dance with a long line of do-si-dos until you exit at Leavenworth Street.

Russian Hill is a pretty, downtown neighborhood and Lombard may be its prettiest block – charming stucco houses stand shoulder to shoulder, and meticulously maintained peninsulas of hydrangeas are surrounded by low hedges to create the curves. It's definitely the busiest street. One does not maneuver tight corkscrews fast. Thus, in summer, tourist vehicles line up for blocks, engines idling, backing up traffic on cross-streets, impeding intersections, waiting to first-gear it down the winding red brick block.

There has been controversy. Block it off? Prohibit cars? Close it on weekends? Deny tourists – funders of the city's most important industry – the free fun-for-the-family experience they came for? One that they'll film on their phones, post on Facebook and show on YouTube or Vimeo through eternity? Do that and they won't be leaving their hearts in San Francisco anymore.

'How,' I asked Dainen Beretski, the second unit director, 'did you ever get permission to shoot here?'

'San Fran's not so hot any more.'

Other cities . . . Other countries . . . tax incentives . . . sweeter deals. The familiar story. 'Still—'

'Some questions are better not asked.' Beretski grinned and half-turned to finish with a guy wearing a jacket over his de rigueur black T-shirt. I took him to be a liaison with the city. But he was smart enough to wear black in case – God forbid – he stepped into an expensive or precious shot. He might go unnoticed.

Beretski's grin looked at home on his angular face. He was tall, thin, blue-eyed, loose and lanky like a Gumby without the bell bottoms. Despite the cold wind, the fog settling like snow on our heads and shoulders, he was only wearing jeans and a sweatshirt, and the sleeves of that were cropped. Each arm looked like it could hoist me over his head and hold me up like a globe on a lamppost, all while he chatted on his cell phone. To both of us, he announced, 'We've got to be out of here by seven. Everything stowed, all vehicles moved. Or—' He drew his finger across his neck. Then he grinned. 'Here's the secret. Open access to the lunch wagon. Not just crew and talent. Neighbors welcome. They love it.'

'Genius!' I over-the-top'd. In the world of up-and-coming, bursting onto the scene, hotter-than-hot envelope pushers and edge players, Dainen Beretski was the supernova. My agent's watch-your-ass-and-your-neck warning might be on target – still, getting a gig in one of his productions was a coup.

I didn't ask about my predecessor and why she wasn't here. Later, I'd find out if she'd left for a family emergency or a personal one – broken engagement or a broken neck. But no way was I going to hex myself on my first day on the set. There was too much to learn. I grabbed coffee and a scone – nothing too gooey or sweet just in case – from the lunch wagon and began glancing at the Side – dialogue, scene description, bare bones need-to-knows – all on a half-page in a booklet I couldn't keep. No full script, nothing on an iPad that could be used to leak the story before the filming was even done. I wasn't surprised when Beretski delegated an assistant to tell me the plot of *Kite Flight*: girl meets boy at Berkeley Kite Festival, moves in with him in San Francisco and finds madcap problems.

Our gag followed a fight with the boyfriend. The girl runs out of her apartment a block away from our set, skirts the Hyde Street cable car at the top of Lombard and ends up on a moving van dolly, a four-foot-square, foot-and-a-half-high rolling wooden platform on four wheels. She has to surf down Lombard till she falls head over heels into a passing truck. A three-part gag.

'Are you the stuntwoman on this?'

I was so intent on picturing the gag I didn't recognize the woman's voice. Then I did one of those what-are-you-doing-here double-takes. 'Aurelia?' Aurelia Abernathy? What *was* Leo's little friend from his Japan days doing here?

'This is so cool. You're doing the stunts. When I saw the notice about this movie shoot here, I figured, "Watch and learn," right? But I didn't dream I'd get to see *you* do the stunts. See *how* you do them. 'S'Kay if I get some coffee? Something to eat?'

I stood, stunned. In the business hustling your way onto a set, even one like this, was frowned upon – how did the production heads know you weren't going to spy and leak secrets? Cadging food was pushing it. She hadn't waited for an answer and the speed with which she downed the first doughnut made me wonder how long it had been since she last ate.

The wind was rustling her short brown curls like beach grass in a storm. Whatever she thought the temperature would be atop this hill, she wasn't prepared for it. Her black tunic with bright green leggings gave her the look of a frog on the way to yoga class. Her polyester sweater (black with green polka dots) screamed looks not warmth. One thing I'd learned about a location set like this: adorable is adorable but icy is forever, or near enough to it. I was decked in sweats over tights, all black like everyone else in the crew, my long red hair stuffed up into a wool cap. 'How's Leo?' Aurelia asked, now sipping coffee.

'Asleep. The doctor saw him yesterday.'

'And said?'

'Bed rest.'

'And he'll be back to normal? Bouncing around like he was in Japan?' She said it with such delighted relief I couldn't help but smile.

'He was bouncing around in Japan?' I said, amazed. The Side was still in my hand. I needed to be studying. But this would be just a tiny, short tidbit from a period Leo had never mentioned.

I hadn't focused on her constant movement, but now her sudden stillness was startling. It made me wonder if it had been she, not Leo, doing the bouncing. 'You know, I didn't know him well,' she said. '"Know" is too strong a word. *Kinda* knew. But yeah, he was very focused – that kind of energy, like he could get all excited about a dog face call—'

Dog face call? Dōgen *face call? Oh, fascicle of Dōgen! Essay of the great thirteenth-century Japanese Zen teacher.* I nodded to her.

'He was the only American at his temple. Maybe the only newbie priest. The old guys had him sweeping and shoveling and hauling stuff and cleaning the toilets all day long. Sitting on his cushion must have been a real break for him.'

'Did you see him back in this country? At his monastery up north?'

She stuffed the end of a cruller in her mouth and chewed. 'The place in the woods? No. I mean, I thought I would when I came back from Japan later, but he didn't let me stay.'

'Really?' That didn't sound like Leo. The monastery was barebones, backwoods. People weren't lining up to get in. Though if she'd been in Japan and didn't know the difference between Master Dōgen and a cocker spaniel, maybe she wasn't monastery material.

'Darcy!' Dainen called sotto voce and motioned me to a plump woman dressed down to movie crew plainness – clothes black and baggy, hair streaked with gray and pulled back into a clasp halfway up the back of her head. Her whole being said: behind the scenes. I followed her into the wardrobe wagon, spent half an hour trying on a yellow print dress and donning the hip pads I'd be wearing and standing while she fitted the dress to hide them so it wouldn't look like the character had gained ten pounds since the previous scene.

'Have to work fast,' she said, mostly to herself, 'to get all these done.' On the rack hung five identical dresses. In case – for the likelihood – that one or two would be ripped beyond salvation with each gag.

By the time I changed back into my own sweatshirt and tights and walked out the light had changed, as if the fog had been vacuumed up. It wasn't quite dawn, but it wouldn't be long. There'd be no action on this set today, which was just as well for me.

'More coffee?' Aurelia popped up at my side.

'Sure.'

In seconds she was back with coffee and going at a cheese Danish. 'What're you doing now?' she said between bites. 'Dainen said it was OK to ask you.'

You asked Beretski? On my first day? I was going to have to deal with this, pronto. But not here. I inhaled very slowly and said, without revealing outrage, 'I'll be studying the Sides and reading over the gag part carefully.'

'Gag? Stunt, huh?'

I nodded. There was still a lot for Dainen to figure out, but that wasn't the kind of information I'd be passing on to an outsider.

As if bouncing foot to foot and drinking coffee without spillage wasn't enough, she eyed the page in my hand. In my family I'd been called Monkey, the wired child, etc., but Aurelia was buzzing at a whole 'nother level. 'There're eight curves on this block,' she said, 'but only three gags?'

'Eight switchbacks, right. But you can't do a gag on every turn. First, it would be almost impossible to set up and to pull off. Second – and even more important – eight gags one after another would look ludicrous. Viewers would be laughing – at us! It would take them right out of the watching-the-movie mode and into hooting and throwing popcorn.'

'But—'

'Or they'd be overwhelmed. Or just get bored.'

'But—'

'Aurelia, this kind of stunt is like an old joke. One, two, three. Set-up, repetition, punch line. Here it's one switchback mild enough to show you the set-up; the second clear enough to expose the looming dangers. Then, boom, the payoff. Frightening . . . terrifying . . . Omigod!'

At the far sidewalk, Dainen stood face-to-face with another man in black, their arms out, pointing down the street. They could have been waltzing. Gaffers were moving boxes on dollies. The lighting crew stood by banks of lights but left the bulbs dark. They wouldn't turn them on until it was time for the run-through.

'How come no lights?' Aurelia asked, following my gaze.

'This time of morning the natural light changes by the minutes. And day to day. This morning we've got fog. Tomorrow it could be clear. Or it could rain. February's an iffy month here. The crew will need to check, but – and this is important – no one wants to irritate the neighbors by shining lights in their bedrooms or running late on the set here. They've already got big trucks.' I nodded at the vans parked on Lombard on the far side of Hyde Street, making things more congested than normal. 'And they've got all of us here before dawn. Notice how quiet people are?'

She was going at the last bite and for a moment the clack of her teeth drummed into the silence. For that moment nearly everyone on the set was staring at Aurelia chewing. She went pink. Then she laughed, but silently. And all around us, gaffers, crew guys, the *scripty*, a.k.a continuity supervisor, and the clutch of neighbors or tourists on the sidewalks were smiling.

Then they were all back to looking at sketches, at retaining walls, checking the slope or walking their dogs. Aurelia was eyeing the light banks.

'That's it, guys! Let's break it down. We've got ten minutes to get clear,' Dainen called. The first loud voice of the morning.

'You just have time to make morning zazen, Aurelia.'

'You coming?'

'I need to talk to Dainen.' I gave her a send-off tap on the shoulder and, in case she missed the point, added, 'See you there.'

I looked around for the stunt coordinator. I wanted to meet him or her. But no likely candidate stood out, and by the time Dainen, the second unit director and thus his boss, finished up, banks of lights had been loaded into trucks, the wardrobe truck was locked and the lunch wagon gone. SUVs with out-of-state plates were waddling around the switchbacks, cell phones and iPads held out of their windows, cars on their tails. And Beretski was double-timing it up the street.

'Dainen! Can you give me the stunt coordinator's number?'

'Don't have one!' he called over his shoulder.

'No phone?'

'No coordinator.'

'Who's—?'

'Me. Double-dutying.'

'Really?' *Dangerous.*

'First day here and you're telling me my job?'

I hesitated, briefly but big time. There are instants that can change your life. It's rare you know it at the moment, but this time I sure did. My whole professional future hung on this job and I'd just put it on the line!

Dainen Beretski was not smiling.

I flashed a grin and said, 'Hey, that's why you hired me!'

A blue car pulled up beside him. Without looking back, he slid in.

TEN

I ran because I was late – I'd miss morning zazen entirely – and to outrace the dread about Beretski and my tentative hold on my job. What were the odds of my being canned on my first day? Hot-shot second unit directors do not like being second guessed, particularly by a stunt double who's been on the job all of two hours.

Panting, I crossed Columbus, skidded to a more zendo-suitable walk at Renzo's closed cafe and found the courtyard flush with more post-morning zazen people than I'd ever seen here. As I veered through the opening between the low stone wall and the building, a burly, wooly bundle of gray – for a moment I took him to be Hudson Poulsson, Leo's driver yesterday, but he wasn't – grumbled past me, jamming a sleeping bag into a wheeled duffle while trying to fold up one of those silvery warmth blankets agencies give the homeless. He nearly sideswiped me, leaving a trail of eau de sweat and wet wool.

A hand – not his – grabbed my arm. 'We've got a problem.' Nezer Deutsch, Leo's doctor. He pulled me toward the zendo door, past Tully Lennox, Lila and Mr Golf Cart, the reporter who had been so outraged at Snell's questioning yesterday morning.

I thought they'd follow, that everyone would. But even the reporter stood, as if transfixed. 'Leo . . .' Deutsch cleared his throat. 'I think someone was poised to attack Mr Garson.'

'Now? Here? Upstairs? Is Leo hurt? What—'

He stared.

'Did you take care of him?'

'The attacker didn't actually get to him.' He stepped back, moving his thin frame as if by remote control. He looked like a creature that hadn't seen the sun in months, and maybe he was. Like someone who needed a long night's sleep before making any decisions. If Leo didn't heal fast we'd have to discuss this medical choice of his. Deutsch cleared his throat. 'Someone was hanging around outside Mr Garson's door.'

'Maybe someone who just wanted to see him?'

'No. It was different.' He seemed uneasy, like he was about to reveal a bad diagnosis, one he couldn't be entirely certain about but which he could not avoid mentioning. 'A person waiting to visit a patient walks heavily up the stairs. They want to give warning, to let the sick person prepare themselves. I've seen this many times in the hospital; people make a noise outside the room. But this, today . . . I didn't hear the footsteps coming up the stairs. The stairs are wooden. Even rubber soles would, uh, clump on them. I only realized later that I'd heard someone; the steps were that soft. And then, later, when I was about to leave – I was still inside the room – I had my hand on the knob, the door several millimeters ajar. I was facing the patient, talking . . . someone rushed across the landing and down the stairs.'

'They went right past you?'

'Behind me.'

'Did you turn around?'

'As I said, they rushed. I turned, but they'd already gone downstairs. I heard the door shut. There was nothing to see. My point' – he paused, pointedly – 'is that this building is a very open place. You should be careful. Take measures.'

'But Leo's OK, right?'

'For now. But there's not much point in my coming to treat him if you're going to leave the door open for public transit.' He stood, arms crossed, his badly cut brown hair unkempt, as if this trip to see Leo had robbed him of the time to comb it. The man was resentment personified. I had the feeling he would clutch his inconvenience and nurture the grudge as long as he could.

'Right!' I whipped behind him, into the building, leaving him to deal with the crowd of Leo's students eager for news – good news – of their teacher. And the reporter, who was just eager.

I took the stairs two at a time. Leo's door was shut.

I knocked. 'Leo?'

He made a noise I chose to translate as 'come in.'

Leo lay on the floor, blankets crumpled around him like discarded Kleenex. His eyelids fluttered almost shut. His skin was moist, sallow.

'Are you OK?' A not-bright question. I knelt down next to his head. No new bruises. 'Leo! Was someone in here?'

'Nezer.'

'The doctor, sure. Anyone else?'

His head rolled side to side as if he was shaking it 'no.' But he could have just been moving it. He squeezed his eyes a couple times as if trying to focus. 'Bathroom.'

'You mean you were trying to get up?'

'Now.'

I helped him roll onto his stomach and then up. For a man who had done thousands of full bows before the altar, rocking back on his heels and springing, in a stately manner, up, the move was almost instinctual and I only needed to put a supportive hand on his back.

Once on his feet, though, instinct and energy vanished. With his arm around my shoulder, mine supporting his back, we turned to the door.

The reporter stood in the doorway, notepad out.

'This is our private—'

'Who attacked you . . . sir?'

Sir!

Leo groaned.

'Do you mind?' I hissed.

'I'm just ask—'

'Out . . . of . . . the . . . way!'

He moved back, reluctantly. I did a quick glide with Leo into the bathroom and pulled the door shut.

Leo propped a hand on the sink, looking considerably steadier than before. 'I can handle this.' He winked.

Or close enough.

I was so relieved I just stood there smiling until he stage-whispered, 'Do you mind?'

'OK, OK.'

I stepped back into the tiny hallway. Once again I was face-to-face with the reporter.

'Roman Westcoff. Call me Ro,' he said, as if proffering a gift.

Everything about the guy said 'on-the-run.' Lanky but no way near muscular. Skin uneven in tone and texture, as if his idea of dinner came from dropping quarters into a slot. Pale hair so short he might have painted his skull. A dark tweed jacket that must have looked great new on its original owner but was now frayed and pocket-sprung from jammed-in pens, tape recorders, lunch maybe. Running shoes.

He kept his head thrust forward as if to catch the words first. It was a narrow head with the features thrusting, too. Narrowed eyes and a protruding nose with a little bulb on the end. And oddly, a touch of cologne that filled me with a nostalgia I couldn't place.

Before I could speak, he broke that spell. 'Yeah, I'm still here. Still waiting for a single word with Mr Garson.'

Single word. Yeah, right! 'Can't you see how sick he is?'

'Answer me one question.'

'Can't you— Oh, hell, what?' I was half listening, ear cocked for the first sound of Leo stumbling, half trying to politely, ridiculously, block out toilet noises.

'Who did this to him?'

'That's your one question?'

'This isn't a game.'

You're telling *me!* A dozen sarcasms rushed forward. All the tension of the last thirty-six hours burst in my skull. 'Get out! Just go!'

'Hey, I thought you Buddhists were big on compassion.'

'We're not big on being patsies.'

'I'm just asking—'

'Ask later. Downstairs!' It was all I could do to not grab him, turn him around and head – not shove – him to the stairs.

'I still have one question.'

'Downstairs!' Now I did reach toward him.

He moved down onto the first step. And stopped. Notebook still out. 'Tell me this: where does Garson-roshi go on Wednesdays?'

'What?'

'Wednesdays, where does he go?'

'Every Wednesday?'

'The last Wednesday of the month. Every month.'

'Those are your questions: who attacked him, something you presume I know but just haven't gotten around to mentioning to anyone. And what does he do at teatime on Wednesdays?'

Sarcasm slipped right off him. 'Your answer?'

'I don't know.'

The toilet flushed. Was Leo signaling me to get rid of Westcoff?

He could hear our voices on this side of the flimsy door. Or was a man in the bathroom just flushing the toilet? Whichever, I needed to get this reporter out of here.

I decided to go with facts. 'Wednesdays? There are a lot of possibilities. Priests meeting. Senior students meeting. Committee meetings. Meetings about the practice of the Practice. The world of emptiness is full of meetings.'

I thought he'd at least smile. Not a twitch. He said, 'Meetings outside the city?'

'Where outside?'

'You tell me.'

'I don't know. No, really. I have no idea.'

'But you will, right? You'll get the answer.' Now he smiled, a knowing little smile, like he'd scooped a bit of me into one of those bulging pockets.

And he probably had. 'Maybe,' I wavered.

'And you'll text. Since I'm the one who pointed this out to you.'

'We'll see.'

Water shot into the bathroom sink. It sloshed against the porcelain. Westcoff's eyes shot to the door. No way was I going to let him get at Leo.

Westcoff turned back toward me and stared long enough to make eye contact. 'I don't give up.'

'Bully for you.'

'Hey, I—'

'Downstairs.'

'I don't—'

'Downstairs. Come on.' As soon as he turned the corner on the landing I called to Leo, 'I'll just be a minute. You OK in there?'

'Yes.' His voice quavered. If he was OK, he wouldn't be for long.

I raced down. Of course, Westcoff was waiting not an inch from the bottom step. 'Trying to grow elephant ears?'

'If I could, I would, even if it meant never getting a decent cap again.' He shot me a grin. It made the bulb on his nose twitch.

I said, 'Were you up upstairs earlier today?'

'Why? What happened?'

'Nothing. Just a question. Which you didn't answer.'

'Come on, you don't run down here to ask about nothing.'

'Were you?'

'Who told you—'

'Were you up there?'

'No, but—'

'Fine. Did you see anyone going up here? I mean, besides the doctor?'

He shook his head, annoyed, as if he should have seen someone, as if it was his right to have had that sighting, as if someone else, a stringer maybe, had been given access to the sight instead.

A board creaked upstairs. Leo trying to make it across the hall without me? I shifted a foot onto the stairs. 'Maybe there was no one here. I just wanted to know. Nothing happened. No missed scoop. So don't be not giving up on this item. Got it?' I know about not giving up, too.

He reached for my arm but restrained himself. 'There's a story here. I will get it. That's the good and bad news for you.'

The bathroom door catches on the sill when it opens. Leo had gotten it that far.

I started up the stairs.

'The good news—' Westcoff called as I hit the landing.

I stopped.

'—is that I'm on this. No one else cares. This attack, it's nothing to the cops. Won't be till your priest gets his head bashed in. Or worse. You can't protect him forever. You've got to flush out the bad guy who did this. And, Darcy, right?'

'Yeah.'

'The bad news, Darcy, is your only ally is me!'

Chances were Westcoff was right. But I didn't have time to dwell on that. In the Bay Area where every day's news could lead with a murder, a mere wounding, even of someone as unlikely as Leo, was hardly big stuff. So why did Westcoff care? 'Shut the door behind you,' I called and raced up the stairs, knowing I'd already waited too long.

ELEVEN

Leo nearly fell out of the bathroom. He'd been hanging onto the doorjamb. He saw me, tumbled, and I grabbed him.

'Good catch!' His voice was a whisper.

'I should've—'

'Illusion.' He meant that the recriminations I was about to launch were useless – things I shouldn't have done, things I might have done but did not, none of which would change anything now. Words to crowd out fear. We had had discussions on this before. He was right. Still, as I had told him, those instants in the recrimination process when, for a split second, in my own mind I had done the right thing, were ridiculously seductive illusions.

'Ridiculously,' he'd repeated.

Now he wasn't saying anything. His breaths were thick and heavy, his skin damp, and he was nearly dead weight in my arms.

With some maneuvering I settled him on his futon, propped him up to drink some water, then eased him down and pulled the covers up.

'Leo—'

'Shocking, huh? Not even sixty years old and . . .'

'The weakness? Yes.'

He waggled a hand.

'Comes and goes, yes.' I interpreted. 'But still . . .'

'Looked better before?'

'True dat.'

He flashed a pale smile at my lack of bedside manner, the lack he'd insisted on in the past. Then, I'd promised him I'd be the one person he could trust, the truth teller. I asked, 'Did the doctor say this might happen? Or to worry if it did?'

'Offered me pain pills—'

'Which you did not take, right?'

'Pain.'

I nodded. Pain, he'd said more than once, can be a tool for concentration. Makes it hard for your mind to wander happily in speculation, to replay scenes of triumph or regret, or hope for fish tacos for dinner when your toe is throbbing. Throb – pay attention. Throb – pay attention. 'There's a limit, though. Even for you.'

'Not there yet.'

'I can call the doctor.'

'Just here . . . Tomorrow.'

Reluctantly, I nodded. So I'd missed any medical advice Dr Nezer Deutsch night have offered and wouldn't get another shot at him till morning. Damn Gracie and her sudden trek to Vegas.

The tea I'd brought him this morning sat untouched. I reached toward it but he stopped me with a glance. I wanted to make him more tea, to help him drink, to straighten his blankets, to do . . . something. I sighed.

'Go.'

But I couldn't. It took all my restraint not to reiterate the dangers of his situation with his assailant running around free to have another go at him. But I'd said it once. He'd considered it as much as he was going to. And yet . . .

I poured water from his pitcher into the cup he hadn't touched.

His eyelids fluttered.

'Leo, tell me one thing.'

His eyes opened. 'Nothing you don't know . . . healing on schedule. No more health chat.'

'Fair enough.'

He eased back, eyes fluttering toward closed.

'Hey, not yet. One thing: tell me where you've been going on the last Wednesdays of the month?'

Nothing changed – his expression, his breathing, the way his body lay. My question had been as far out from leftfield as Ro Westcoff's to me. Did Leo even grasp it? I was about to rephrase it when he said, 'No.'

'No?'

'Can't tell you.'

'Why not?' The words were out before I could stop myself.

'Not now.'

'You can't tell me anything?'

'Trust me.'

'I do, but Leo, this situation is dangerous!'

'Yes.' He struggled in the blankets. I reached to help but he waved me off and managed to prop himself on one elbow. 'Go. Stay with your mother. I don't want you here.'

'Because it's dangerous?'

'Go.' He let out the word with an exhausted breath, and with it collapsed back down on the futon.

I said, 'Fat chance.'

He didn't answer, didn't shrug a reply. Just let his eyes close. This interview was over.

I straightened the blankets over him and walked out. I left his door open, as I would my own across the hall. But one thing I knew was that he would do what he would do. And he wouldn't answer any question he chose not to, which meant he was not going to tell me another thing.

Frustrated, irritated and not a little unnerved, I decided to do the sensible thing and get coffee.

The courtyard was emptying – people had jobs to go to. Renzo had a cafe to run. As I stepped outside I spotted Snell walking toward Columbus, looking straight ahead of him. At Lila Suranaman. From my angle of vision I couldn't be sure, but his interest appeared not entirely professional. She was, of course, a strikingly lovely woman with a sultry sway to her butt, which was what Snell seemed intent on investigating.

Beyond the gate from the other direction men's voices sparred. One low, one loud, rasping. Familiar.

My brother was chewing out the poor homeless guy from our courtyard.

'Let him be, John!'

He did a double-take, muttered something and, to my surprise, did indeed let the man go on his way.

And turned on me. 'He was sleeping outside your window! He could have—'

'He didn't—'

'You don't know who he is.'

'Leo probably does. John, he's not the first man to sleep here.

The courtyard's protected and warm, at least as warm as San Francisco gets in February. And – you know this is true – Renzo probably slips these guys a cup of coffee and something to eat and checks them out in the process.'

'Still—' It so pained my brother to admit he was wrong.

'You want to do something for Leo? For me? Then keep an eye on Leo while I do just what you want me to – go to Mom's.' By which I meant the beach a couple blocks from there, but that I didn't specify.

What could he say?

I put out my hand for his car keys.

Half an hour later I pulled up in front of the house I grew up in. Mom was on the phone, but Duffy, the Scottie still known as 'Darcy's dog,' raced up to me, wagging his stub of a tail. I'd inherited him on a location set a couple years ago when his previous owner made an emergency exit minutes before the sheriff arrived. Duffy had flown back to New York with me and made more friends there than any decently reserved Scottish Terrier would tolerate. He accompanied me to movie sets, a couple times getting his own director's chair. And then I'd moved back to San Francisco and he'd found Mom. Whatever any person thought about him being 'Darcy's dog,' in Duffy's mind I was a courier who had guided him to his true abode. Mom was home a lot. All of us adult kids and now my sister Katy's teenagers stayed here at times. Someone was always coming through the door, allowing him to pretend he didn't want to be fussed over. There was always a pot of beef stew scenting the kitchen. On the couch in front of the television there were two indentations.

I grabbed his leash.

Mom put down the phone. 'Want company?'

'Sure,' by which I meant 'no,' and yet when you're the last of seven, you never turn down the chance of your mother's full attention.

Unwilling to display pleasure, Duffy trotted face straight-forward between us, alert for vermin threatening the sidewalks of San Francisco, prepared to protect his herd of two from the peril of salt water.

The briny smell of ocean grew stronger as we neared the

beach. Damp wind scraped my skin as if shearing off the layers of excess. I thought of all the times I'd taken this walk as a babbling, cartwheeling child, a younger teenager desperate to say the clever, the astute, the adult thing to my four-years-older brother as we ran to the dunes for 'serious talk.' After Dad died, I'd walked here with Gracie, when she couldn't talk at all or couldn't stop the flood of words, and taken short, uneasy walks with Mom, when she just stared out into the sea. When I came home after avoiding the city for nearly twenty years, the whole family built a fire on a secluded part of the beach and roasted marshmallows.

I unsnapped the leash. Duffy stayed where he was; he'd never acknowledge a strap controlled his behavior.

Mom is a listener. I think I'm her favorite, but I suspect all my sibs believe that of themselves. Still, Mom and I sense the signals of each other's movements. At times like this we jig and jag as one, chat and walk together in the pool of silence. It wasn't till we crossed The Great Highway onto the sand that she said, 'So?'

'So?'

'So, woman comes to walk on the beach with a dog. Woman's got something on her mind.'

The wind shoved a clump of hair in my face. I pushed the red curls back behind my ear, pretending they would stay there. 'I'd decided my career was over and I'd have to go to L.A. or Toronto. Then, out of the blue, I landed a great gig. And now I've probably blown it.'

She made a come sign with her hand and I gave her the rundown on the gag, Dainen Beretski's renown, and of the agent's assistant's warning, toned down in case I didn't get canned, and my parting comments to Beretski.

Mom nodded. There was nothing to say. And she didn't say it! She focused on a fast breaker spewing water within inches of our feet. Neither of us moved. It had been a game when I was a kid. Then the rule was the one who chose the wave couldn't move. We sloshed home a lot.

'You haven't mentioned Leo.'

'Surely John told you.'

'Surely.' She smiled in that way she had of acknowledging

the idiosyncrasies of one of her offspring and the annoyance of another without herself taking sides. 'And?'

My phone rang.

'You want to—'

'It can go to voicemail. Leo. Someone attacked him. I can't tell whether he's too out of it to be worried or . . .'

'Too Leo?'

'Exactly.'

'The cops sent a crime scene unit. I guess I should be glad for that much. But they're not really interested, and a reporter's *too* interested. He's got a bug up his ass about Leo having some meeting one Wednesday a month. I asked Leo and he won't say what it is. I mean, Mom, he's been bludgeoned and he refuses to reveal his mid-week assignations.'

'Maybe that's what they are.'

'Oh, I don't think—'

'He's a cute guy, Darce.'

I stopped dead and turned toward her.

She grinned. 'Gracie and I agree.'

'You discussed Leo's desirability with my sister?'

She laughed. 'I did. I said, "If I were younger . . ." Gracie said she *is* younger.'

Jesus! 'And?'

'Well, you know, Gracie's got a lot to do.'

It was the family joke that there would always be enough in the way of epidemics to keep Gracie too busy to buy a house, clean her car, get a life.

I was still staring at her as Mom said, 'You Buddhists aren't celibate. He's a middle-aged single man. You'll soon be his age. Are you planning to be on the shelf then? So, why wouldn't he be seeing someone? He doesn't have to tell you about it. And certainly not a reporter.'

My phone rang again. Mom hesitated again.

'It's not John's ring. It'll keep.' It could, I thought, be Beretski, in which case it wasn't likely to improve my day. 'And there's this girl Leo met in Japan – she's not Japanese – who he wouldn't let into the monastery when he was abbot up there. And you know that monastery's not exactly a spa. Last I saw her she was slithering out the zendo door.'

'Well, case in point! He's a cutie. I always wondered if you—'

I crossed my hands in a NO! sign. 'He's my teacher. I need to make my romantic mistakes elsewhere.'

'Jes sayin'!'

This was not the conversation I'd intended to have. And not one I intended to continue. I glanced around for Duffy, ready to call him back from danger or a fracas. But he was right there between us, providing not a bit of distraction. I turned to Mom. 'So, where's Gracie? Her secretary said she's in Vegas but she doesn't know which hotel. At some conference but she hadn't decided what. That's flaky, even for Gracie.'

'Incommunicado? At least you know she'd not off with Leo.'

'Mom!' That trip of Gracie's was peculiar but I should have known Mom wouldn't say so. And yet there was something a little off in her tone. 'Mom?'

She took the leash and bent down to attach it. Duffy stiffened. We wouldn't be crossing the street for another eighth of a mile. Looking at Duffy's back, Mom said, 'She's been . . . I don't know . . . off. She's never gone off like that before, at least not since the city cut funding for the flu study and that was five years ago.'

'Early menopause?'

Mom snapped to standing, 'Jesus, Mary and Joseph! Don't let her know you even had that thought. And no. Maybe this weekend away was just what she needed.' She looked pointedly at me. 'I'm not speaking of it.'

I nodded. Me bring up hormonal fading with my doctor sister? Fat chance.

My phone rang again. I looked questioningly at Mom. 'Go ahead,' she said.

With relief all around, I answered it, just as it was clicking off.

Then I checked for messages. Two. Both from the same number.

Dainen Beretski.

In the first, he said, 'Call me.'

The second message was the same, but the words were more clipped.

This wasn't an issue I wanted to deal with in the wind, on the sand by the whoosh of traffic on The Great Highway. I pocketed the phone, walked back to the house, hugged Mom, who was saying something about making a new pot of stew because John and Gary might swing by late tonight after something or other out this way, and headed for the privacy of the car.

TWELVE

I slid into the car outside Mom's house and called Dainen Beretski. It sounded like I'd caught him in a war zone. 'Beretski!'

'Darcy Lott!' I shouted, feeling like Alexander Graham Bell.

'Heard you're interested in moving up to stunt coordinator. How about it?'

Really? Wow! WOW! 'Yes.'

'Meet me in the war room. Seven o'clock. Hang on.' More shouting. 'Broadway and wointinh.'

'What?'

'Mowtinooosh.'

Damn, I could not miss out on the big change of my career because I muffed the address. 'Street number?' I asked, hoping the place was on Broadway rather than mowtinooosh.

He repeated it, clearly. I heard, hung up and whipped back in the house to tell Mom.

I parked John's car outside the zendo at quarter after five, hurried upstairs to check on Leo, thank John for keeping an eye on him in my absence and ask if he would stay this evening. Leo was sleeping quietly and, across the hall on my futon, John was snoring.

At 5:30 p.m. I stood silent for a minute, then stepped into the courtyard and hit the clappers three times to announce the evening sitting, walked into the meditation hall, replaced the clappers, bowed to the altar and took the front seat – not the abbot's seat which is never covered by anyone but Leo, but the cushion on the far side of the altar. I sat facing into the room.

The size of evening zazen group seemed barely affected by Leo's attack. I'd suspected Roman Westcoff might be trolling, but apparently his 'never give up' gave up in the face of another forty minutes of sitting cross-legged. The only addition was Lila Suranaman from a strip club on Broadway, looking smaller and more nervously out of place than ever as she walked in. She bowed to the cushion nearest me, sat, swirled to face the wall and exhaled slowly, as if she'd cloaked herself in safety, at least for a while.

When the *doan* – timekeeper – rang the bell at quarter to six, there were eight people in the zendo. A couple hurried in minutes later and took spots near the door. A bit after 6:15 p.m. – minutes before the end of the sitting – a thick man in a dark hoodie poked his head in, surveyed the room and left.

My breath caught. The hoodie?

I wanted to race through the door after him.

I eased to my feet and walked quietly – not that 'quietly' exists when moving in a silent room – past the altar, pausing to bow, then behind people sitting on the far row of zabutans and through the door.

The hallway was empty. As quietly as I could, I raced up the stairs and peered into both bedrooms, the bathroom and even the closet.

Nothing untoward.

Downstairs, the bell rang. Through the door I heard the rumble of moving bodies and the scraping of chairs as people got up and prepared for final bows. Then I heard the final chant, dissonant voices merged sweetly by the distance. I hurried back upstairs and glanced in Leo's room again. He looked to be asleep, but a watery smile played on his lips.

I checked my hair and face, changed the black T-shirt I'd been wearing all day for a cleaner version. John grunted, rolled over but did not wake. I left him a note.

The zendo was dark, the hallway dim, and even the street seemed after-work empty until I spotted Tully Lennox haltingly hurrying toward me as if half of him opposed the trip. He glanced over his shoulder and then toward the empty courtyard, seemed relieved, hesitated and kept coming. The man reminded me of Duffy about to snatch a piece of stew meat from a plate abandoned on the floor.

I stepped out into the courtyard just as Lila stood up beside a planter box, pausing to check a Christmas cactus she'd planted as a gift to the center.

Outside the courtyard wall, on the sidewalk, well behind Tully,

Renzo raised a palm to stop me. And so I watched tall, tentative Tully Lennox approach waiflike Lila. I couldn't hear his words. She seemed to be straining to catch them. But the storyline was clear. He didn't put his arm around her shoulder, though everything in his stance showed his urge to. They walked toward Columbus Avenue, not touching, but in step and close to each other as if the air between them was touching. And as one, their shoulders relaxed.

'Nice, huh?' Renzo said a minute later.

I nodded.

'I'm going to bring the abbot soup and John dinner.'

'Renzo, what did you do with your life before we moved in here and took it over?'

The second unit production room was not on Lombard Street, or within walking distance of our location on Russian Hill, of course. The movie company had done well to get permission to leave their trucks there overnight in an area on the route to downtown and jammed with tourists. The city wants movies made here. San Franciscans love movies that show their city, and even more their neighborhoods. They just don't want to give up parking spaces to get them.

So the production room was inconveniently blocks away. It huddled in a low brick building a couple blocks from San Francisco Bay, a place that preserved the cold. The walls were insulated only by the printed-out lists for various crews. They covered one full and sizeable wall on the bay side of the room and two on interior walls. The remaining wall formed a backdrop for desks and clutter. And the middle of the room was stacked with cameras, banks of lights, individual lights and a set of rails on which a camera would ride to parallel the action.

There weren't enough windows; they hadn't been open. As I made my way across the room the smell of lunch meat and sweet rolls gave way to a hint of sneaked tobacco. On a table someone had sketched figures in grease pencil. Nearby, someone had used a glue gun. The smells were momentarily distinct and then interwoven like strands in a game of cat's cradle.

I wished I could scan the overall storyboards for the movie to get a sense of the number and complexity of gags in *Kite Flight*. The Lombard gag was huge, but there were a number of smaller ones. If I worked things right, *Kite Flight* could keep me in work for weeks. But there was no way that info would be posted on the walls of our production room where any of us could go rogue and leak it before filming even finished.

Dainen Beretski's limber form was angled over a desk as he peered at the call sheet with a woman holding a pad and a digital recorder, her cell phone poking out from the pocket of a fisherman's vest. On the vest's back was a hook, presumably to hang it from a peg. She had a ring of keys attached to it by a carabiner. I couldn't see what she'd done to the keys to keep them from jangling. She had to be the *scripty,* obsessively keeping track of everything every actor, every setting, plus the weather does at every stopping point. She sighed. 'We can't trust the weather here. We have to start earlier or we're going to have scenes blinking from fog to sun to wind blowing down everything in sight.'

'Can't put toe to ground before five, Margo. It's in the permit. You got a problem, talk—'

'Never mind. I've always got a problem. That's what continuity is.' Her voice was grumpy but her stance was live and let live, quite the achievement in a job where she could catch ninety-nine errors – actor wearing a different shirt from the last shot, different belt, different stud earring, no ring on a finger that had worn one before washing, a car parked inches closer to a hydrant, a flowering plant that had dropped half its buds overnight, a passing street car halfway through the intersection when shooting stopped but absent when it resumed – and all anyone would remember would be the one she missed.

'Darcy!' Beretski proclaimed. 'Everyone, this is Darcy Lott, our savior!'

Savior is not a good role, longevity-wise. 'Wow,' I said, 'all jobseekers should get that welcome.' I near-matched his volume. I've played this in this kind of ballpark before.

Behind him, the scripty looked skeptical.

I prompted, 'You said you needed stunt coordination help . . .'

'Right. This is too big a project for me to be second unit director and stunt coordinator, too. I can't be into the details of the set-up for each stage of the gag the way you need to, you know? I've got to be dealing with Margo,' he nodded at the continuity woman, 'and Barb with her press releases, and then, jeez, just liaising with our location manager, who's liaising with the head of the neighborhood organization at this very moment and the city and MUNI and – you won't believe this – the bike coalition that wants to send five hundred people down Lombard one night in the middle of our shoot. Can you guess how much trash there'll be, even though they swear there won't be as much as a tissue. Margo's about to go nuts. It's crazy . . . crazy!'

'By which you mean normal? Maybe a teensy bit more?'

He started to protest, then didn't. 'Yeah. And a bit.'

'What do you want me to do?'

'I've seen your details,' he said, mostly to himself. 'No stunt coordinator gigs.'

'True. I've assisted twice.'

'Fabulous. OK. Yes. I need you to check over the plans. See if you spot anything Jess overlooked. You know, check the equipment, check the set-up. Do the trial run.'

The trial – the run where you can break your neck if everything's not in the proper place and tied down tight.

'Big job. How long would I have?'

'We're scheduled for five a.m.'

Tomorrow? 'Tomorrow?'

'Yeah.'

Tomorrow! 'Not possible. I'm really sorry.' More than he knew! 'I'd love to work with you, to learn, to be part of this great gag series . . .' I was laying it on, but from his expression, not too heavily. 'But a stunt coordinator's the last line of safety and there's no way I could guarantee that between now and daybreak.' Meaning, we had a potential liability issue.

'You've got the whole night.'

'Dainen, it's *night*! You want me out with banks of lights shining in the neighbor's windows?' I didn't mention sleep; I knew better than that.

'Second that, Dainen!' shouted a guy I took to be the location producer, the guy who'd be dealing with those 3:00 a.m. neighbors.

'OK, OK, the day after tomorrow. But we've only got the street till Monday. We don't have any slack.'

Safety isn't slack! But tell that to the money guys. 'Let me go over the storyboard, check where things are.' Meaning: *Let me see if this gargantuan amount of work is within the realm of the possible for six people, much less one.*

Beretski put a hand on my arm and lowered his voice. 'Look, these gags on Lombard, this sequence, is the heart of the movie. If it doesn't go, the whole project's dead. Every one of us will be out of work. Guillermo worked his ass off negotiating with the city to get the access we've got. There's a reason no one else has done gags like these on Lombard. And Darcy, we will never, ever, under any circumstances, get access again. And—'

Beretski's cell rang. He eyed it but didn't answer. I gave him a point for that. His mouth moved like he was chewing over his options, tasting the truth, wanting to swallow it. He spit it out. 'I thought I could handle it all – stunt coordinator and second unit director. I was fucking wrong.'

Behind him the continuity woman's whole body sighed. It said: *Finally!* It said: *We told him!*

Without moving, I took in the room. No one had a phone at the ready. No papers or clothes rustled. The whole place looked like Pompeii. Their eyes were on Dainen, as if waiting for the next shoe to drop. And on me, the person who'd made the great Dainen Beretski admit he was wrong. If I did that and then walked out . . . bad, bad, bad for everyone.

That moment stretched like a pocket in time, and I saw the circle of my options. Nix the job and take the muttering that I wasn't good enough, smart enough, brave enough. That nearing forty – 100 in stunt years! – I'd lost it. I was over the hill, sliding down the side where grass goes to die.

If I nixed, Dainen would get someone with less of a resume, who knew zip about this gag sequence – at least I'd eyeballed it this morning – who was maybe less careful, who would make things more dangerous for the stunt double . . .

. . . The stunt double who was me!

Dainen muttered, 'Budget.'

I knew what he meant – he'd been hired because he'd assured

them he could do both jobs. They'd save money. Now he couldn't admit he was over his head.

If I nixed, I wouldn't be part of the production team, the stunt team, the movie, the whole thing that I loved. I'd have to move to Toronto or wherever, and leave Leo exposed. I'd . . .

I should have considered it logically, dispassionately, sensibly, but I said, 'We'll make it work.'

THIRTEEN

I hung around the production office, checking the equipment, going over the storyboard for the whole sequence of gags down Lombard. I focused on the first of the three gags, eyed the stills of the site, checked in with the unit manager, gave him my agent's contact number and looked over the list of equipment he'd bought or rented, scanning down quickly for items like hard foam and duct tape, things I might not expect to need but would in a hurry if I did. Neither of the location assistants was still here; I texted the senior of the two to ask for quirks or problems at the location. If they'd been here – if I had time – I'd have checked with the prop master, the prop maker, the key scenic artist and the lighting crew. When I walked out of the war room it was nearly eleven.

The streets had turned gray. Fog, which had been just a suspicion hours earlier, clung damp to my arms. I yearned for wipers to clear my eyes the way the ones of John's car had handled the windshield when they were new. My T-shirt was about four layers inadequate. I ran to the car, raced the engine and hoped for heat. In the shivering interim I texted Renzo.

Of course he was up. The man never slept.

And of course he'd ring the bell for the morning sitting. He'd assured me the last time I'd needed him to cover for me at the zendo while I raced to a location set that he was investing good luck in me, hoping – no, *expecting*, he'd insisted – that I would rise to be second unit director of the next movie here and set the action outside his cafe.

'With a cameo for you?' I'd asked.

'Sexy Italian? Gotta boost the box office.' He'd winked, sexily.

I parked by the zendo. Pacific Avenue was empty, the street-lights puff balls against the blanket of gray. Even in running shoes my footsteps drummed on the sidewalk and when I walked into our courtyard I could see a dark shape shift in the protected corner. Someone in a sleeping bag, I hoped. That or the biggest rat in the city's history. Amazing that John hadn't swept him out, man or rodent. It made me uneasy as I unlocked the double doors and slipped inside.

Upstairs, Leo was sleeping, breathing easily. All to the good. John, however, was not. He was standing in the doorway of my room, the floor littered with white cardboard and paper bags. It smelled like a *trattoria*.

'Anything left?' I whispered, stepping inside and pushing the door shut. The room has just enough space for a futon, dresser, closet, a pile of books. Two occupants is one too many.

'Hardly,' John hissed back. 'I've worked shifts shorter than this. Been here so long my phone's gone dead. Your note said you'd be back hours ago—'

It hadn't. But no point getting into that. Still, I took a bit off the balance of the debt I owed him for this. 'Thanks.'

But John had plenty of complaining left in his tank. 'There's no food in this place. How do the two of you survive? Would it kill you to . . . Take-out menus at the very minimum!'

It's hard to project outrage when whispering. I restrained the urge to grin.

'Or a bottle of *Powers*.'

Oh. 'Yeah, a nip of the Irish would have helped you. Sorry. Truly. How's Leo?'

'Fine. Got himself up a couple times. Ate soup – soup that Renzo brought him.'

'Did the doctor come?'

'Yeah, but not till Leo called.'

'Leo called?' I didn't know whether to be angry with the ever-grudging Nezer Deutsch or relieved that Leo was in good enough shape to manage the phone.

'Insisted. Guess, all those years in charge of the monastery, he learned how to give an order, no nonsense. That squirrely doctor of his was banging on the door here in half an hour. I told Leo, I said, "Listen, I know medics. I can find you someone a damned sight better." But he told me to mind my own business.'

'Leo said that?'

'Not in words.'

'Did he spit, glare, stick out his tongue?'

'Look, I've done hundreds, thousands of interrogations. I know what "I'll deal with him" means.'

'What'd the doctor say?'

'To me? Nada. Waited till I was in the loo to sneak out.'

'Sneak?'

'Stomp fast. Out the door before I could zip up.'

Good save, John.

A grin escaped John's clenched lips. 'Leo said, loud enough so I heard, "Get yourself here at seven-thirty. That's a.m." Deutsch must've started to bitch. Next thing I hear is Leo: "Nope! Just be here." Some doctor! Jeez, Darce, the whole city of San Francisco – can't Leo do better? Doesn't he have insurance? Everybody in California can have goddamned medical insurance now!'

'We'll find out when the ER bill arrives. Needless to say, I owe you. Meal on me, place of your choice.'

'That and a weekend in Vegas.'

I wanted to retort: maybe you can find Gracie there. But I really did not want to get into the sudden idiosyncrasies of my sister with him now. I reached over and gave my brother an awkward hug.

Then I turned off the light and watched through the window till he was out of the courtyard. I stood there vaguely wondering if I was beginning to channel him.

Which was how come I was still there when the guy who'd been huddled in the courtyard got up, walked to our door, must have tried it, though I couldn't hear any rattle, beat it out to the street and disappeared.

I fished out my phone and punched in John's number.

He didn't answer. As he'd complained minutes ago, his battery was dead.

I raced out of the zendo building at quarter to five in the morning on Thursday and just about fell over Lila Suranaman, huddled in the nearest corner, her long dark hair quivering in the breeze, her arms, in the sweatshirt and pants she always wore here, wrapped around her for warmth there was no way they could provide.

'Early,' she said.

Zazen wouldn't start for two hours!

Her eyes flickered toward the door. Of course, she wanted to wait inside. It was cold and dark out here and someone was snoring in the far corner of the courtyard. Was this a different sleeper or had fear of John only moved him till John drove away last night? If this had been a movie, melodramatic music would be playing.

Thoughts flashed in my head: I don't have time for this.

Lila's been in worse spots dancing for dollars on Broadway. Surely. Or leaving there to walk here. And the country she escaped to come to America and end up slinging her body around a pole – she'd known danger there, right? None of which makes it any warmer now.

I can't afford to be late on the set, today of all days.

If I let her wait inside . . . Hell, I could turn on a light in the zendo and let her sit on a zafu. She's not going to tuck the Buddha under her arm and make a run for it.

Can't do it. Not with Leo asleep upstairs.

I have to decide if the stunts can really work on Lombard. I can't—

I grabbed her arm and hurried her down to Renzo's Caffe where Renzo was just turning on the lights.

Minutes later I was envying her as I raced through the foggy dark for the muted lights of the lunch wagon atop Lombard Street. The wind was moving, not gusting, but moving just enough to batter skin with new smacks of fog. Coffee – the lunch wagon's being nowhere near Renzo quality – can only do so much. The techs and gaffers and an odd clutch of neighbors or groupies stood in that jittery state between conked out and decently awake.

'Can you set up the lights, on that low bank over there?' I asked one of the gaffers. 'I'm going to need it close to the outer wall on that first curve.' The curves were banked and edged with cement walls high enough to keep all but the most errant drivers from bouncing into the shrubbery, but low enough to outline the hydrangeas and greens in the landscaped elbows that created the curves. I had a hooded flat-sided light to check the bricks and a good close-up camera.

'Hey, I heard you got a big promotion! Way to go!'

I turned. There was Aurelia, inches from my back. *You startled me!* But stunt doubles don't do startled, not unless it's scripted. 'Thanks. You're here early.' I kept walking toward the curve.

'Lots to learn, right?'

'Hmm.' I'd forgotten about her urgent urge to be a stunt double. Truth be told, I'd forgotten about *her* and her huge pre-dawn bursts of energy. I did not have time—

'Is this it, this set-up? What're you—'

'Checking for integrity.' *Trying to find a way to make these three gags even possible before the permit window closed on us.* I motioned at Lombard Street with its red brick pavement and eight switchbacks. 'The street's meant for traffic, not for gags. I may end up covering the bricks with that rubber back there' – I motioned toward the truck – 'to slow the descent so we don't go flying—'

'Isn't that what we want?'

'It's how we want it to *appear*. Death-defying made safe – your stunt coordinator at work.'

She nodded so eagerly her brown curly hair bounced.

'We can add the brick look in post-production.' I squatted down in front of the curve, my back to her, hoping she'd take the hint.

'So we have more control?'

'So we don't land up in the shrubbery in every take on every scene.'

'Because of the neighbors?'

I gave up. It'd be faster to answer than to deal with not answering. 'Partly, though the company will restore the garden and anything else we run over. But we've got continuity to consider. We can't be breaking branches on ten tries and on the take have the stunt double landing on bare sticks.'

'Darcy . . .' Her tone was different.

'Yes.'

'You're going to be watching the trial runs, right? You'll need to watch someone doing them, right?'

'Hmm.'

'Well, how about me?'

I should have seen it coming. I *had* seen it, just not coming this soon, and not coming to me. 'Listen, this gag is much trickier than it looks—'

'I'm tougher than I look. I can do this trial run. Look at these muscles.'

I didn't. 'Plus we've got a tight schedule. You don't want to—'

'I worked out every day. Weights. Ran when I could. Did chin ups in my room. I made it my business to come out in good shape.'

'Aurelia, I'm sure you did. No, really. You've got a great future. It's just not now. You don't want to screw up the first time you try. And – this is key – you don't want to cost the company money. Use this to watch and learn. Wait—'

'Wait! I've waited the entire year. I . . . Shit!' She slammed her paper cup onto the table, sending dark brown waves over it and the sidewalk, and stalked off down Lombard, losing the effect of her angry exit in the back and forth, back and forth of the switchback road.

If I hadn't been so focused on the roadway issues, I'd have been stunned. Or furious. Or maybe I'd have laughed as a couple of the techs were doing. As it was, I was glad she was gone. I figured I'd deal with her later.

Famous last words.

For now there was the wall, the cant of the bricks, sixteen-degree grade of the cutbacks, the speed of the dolly as it rounded the curve. We would film one curve at a time. The true speed wouldn't change; the appearance of faster and faster would hinge on post-production changes and the acting that made it believable. I'd be doing the gag but it would be the actress's face showing the reactions. Still, precision was essential. An arm not far enough out on the curve would blow the whole effect. A bounce at a spot that could not have been saved at top speed . . . A brick in the road angled up that would catch a wheel on the dolly . . . If we got the first two gags in the can tomorrow and the final one Monday . . . If we had everything perfect . . . the equipment, the weather, the actress, me . . .

I eyed the bricks, the switchbacks, the narrow sidewalks, the railings and spikes. I considered, and made notes.

When I finally looked up night had vanished, dawn had floated by and the laboratory feel of the dark street was replaced by the flurry of the *grips* rolling the banks of lights back into trucks, the lunch wagon closing and half-hushed frantic voices battling for space.

But mine was the one Dainen Beretski acknowledged. 'So?'

I sighed. 'No way.'

'What?'

'There is no way to do three complicated gags in a week when we've only got this space for two hours a day.'

He nodded, as if what he'd really wanted from me was confirmation, or a miracle.

I offered the latter. 'But, this might work. Send a wheeled board down, slowly, with cameras shooting all four directions. Do three slow shoots – one for each gag, maybe two for the last. Stunt double or actress if you want. Shot of the dolly, the wheels rattling around on the bricks like grocery cart wheels when they're stuck. And then we can get a mobile slant set up and fill it in in the studio.'

'I don't think . . .'

Beside us, lights were brightening, shades were being pulled. Above us, on Leavenworth, truck engines were rumbling into action.

I held my breath.

Dainen considered. 'I don't know . . . I don't want to be the one to let down Geoffrey . . .'

Geoffrey Bates, the producer.

'Geoffrey moved heaven and earth to get Lars.'

Lars Larsson, the location manager.

'Lars had to promise the city his first born. Promised the neighbors his balls.'

'He must've needed them to negotiate this.'

'You don't know the half of it. Darcy, are you sure . . .'

'Absolutely.'

'I'll put it to Geoffrey. I'll call you after.'

'OK,' I said, cloaking my red-hot excitement in the gray cape of professionalism and heading down the hill.

It wasn't till I'd run two more blocks, sufficiently far enough away from the set, that I let out a whoop. This gag stunt sequence was going to get noticed, maybe even awards – with Dainen Beretski in charge, *probably* awards. If there was a better solution than mine, Dainen would have found it. He was going to present my solution to the producer. I was going to get credit on the roll!

I wanted to call . . . Everyone! 'Biggest thing since I moved back to San Francisco!' 'Dainen Beretski!' I wanted to shout to my friends in the business.

But it was not yet eight in the morning. Plus, I didn't dare hex things by cheering too soon.

But Leo would be awake. He'd be happy.

And my agent! Beyond ecstatic. I stopped, texted, then ran on, not tiring but gaining energy, as if from the friction of the joy flowing through me.

I didn't see the flashing red lights till I crossed Broadway.

FOURTEEN

I ran full out toward the zendo. Cars were all but stopped on Columbus Avenue. Both northbound lanes were blocked and traffic had been shifted left into a southbound lane. One lane each way. Flashers blinked off cars like blood splatter. A siren rose to a screech then fell silent. Like they do every night, one after another. Leo and I give them no more notice than a street light flickering. They don't concern us. Until they do.

Leo! He was fine when I left. Renzo was there. John. What could have happened?

An ambulance shrieked around the corner onto Pacific Avenue. On the corner the door to Renzo's Caffe was stuck open. Tables empty, chairs flung back and abandoned. One was overturned. The aroma of coffee flowed through the doorway, flashing normality that didn't exist. I ran on toward the zendo.

By the courtyard entrance a cluster of people looked linty red in the ambulance lights. Two SFPD guys were attaching crime scene tape, blocking off the sidewalk to the east.

One – young, Asian, male – moved in front of me. 'Sorry, ma'am. You can't—'

'What's going on here?' I yelled over the roar of the idling ambulance.

'We're setting up a cordon. You can't—'

'Hey. I live here. In the zendo. With the abbot. In there . . .' I pointed to the courtyard.

'ID?'

I pulled out my wallet, bypassed the Screen Actors' Guild card I'd taken to the set and flipped to my driver's license. 'The abbot, Leo Garson – is this about him?' My heart was beating so hard my ribs were shaking. In the eternity before the cop spoke, dread filled me – no subject, no words, just smoky cold fear.

'Can't say, ma'am.'

Two paramedics walked quickly back to the ambulance. One

pulled open the rear door. Roman Westcoff left the cluster and slid in behind them to peer into the ambulance and back-scurried as they pulled out the stretcher.

Westcoff? Here again?

Two patrol cars idled in the street, the three engines slightly out of sync, buzzing and grumbling in an alternating beat, the sound bouncing off the glass in the boutiques and offices across the street and back against the metal vehicles. I felt like I was in a kettle drum. Night-cold air battled with the hot gust from the ambulance.

'What happened?' I demanded of Westcoff as the paramedics raced the wheeled stretcher through the gateway. Tully Lennox, standing across from me, looked close to tears, his normally pale face dead white.

'What? Dammit, Roman!'

'Ro! Assault,' he said, his eyes on the action behind the court-yard wall.

I leaned over the wall, aware that the cop would come at me and he did, but not in time to keep me from seeing the paramedics bending over a body cloaked in something dark. The courtyard was still dark, the building blocking the sun. Shards of red from the patrol car flashers spit between onlookers and plants and speckled the action.

Why would Leo have come down here? Did he insist on going to zazen? Could he have managed that, even with help?

'Is it Leo?'

'Dunno.'

I grabbed his arm and turned him. 'What *do* you know? Besides your preferred nickname, *Ro*?'

He shook free and shot a glance back at the scene as if to freeze it for later consideration. 'Nine-one-one call seven minutes ago. Woman attacked.'

'Woman? Not Leo.' A gush of relief swept through me. Then shame. And more relief. 'Which woman?'

'No name. Not Aurelia Abernathy. I was looking for her and this woman's nothing like her.' He focused on me with sudden interest. 'You know these people. Who's not here?'

I scanned the group of morning people, regulars huddled together in their communal silence, as if refusing to move the event into words would forestall its reality. If Renzo had been here, he'd tell me.

Tully Lennox had moved apart from the others, his arms tight against his ribs, his dark jacket pulled taut around his beanpole body. His expression – horror, disbelief, grief – said it all. 'Lila?' I asked, softly.

His response was between a nod and a shiver.

'What happened? I know you care about her. I saw you meet her here last night. What is this?'

'I . . . don't know. I came to see her . . . here, at zazen. We'd . . . a couple times . . . had coffee . . . not gone together . . . been at the cafe, both of us, after zazen. Renzo saw us walk in – he knows it wasn't a date.'

I don't care if you two dated. 'You thought you could run into her this morning?' I prompted.

'Here.' He wasn't looking at me; his gaze had never left her, on the pavement in the courtyard, lying still between the paramedics. 'She was here, at zazen.'

'This morning?' Half an hour ago?

'Yes. Like she does. I left first today, like I do. Walked down to Renzo's and . . . She was screaming. All of a sudden, she was screaming! I ran back here and a man was smashing her. He had her like this—' He grabbed my shoulders. He was shaking me, hard.

I broke free, shocked at how much stronger he was than I'd have guessed.

'Sorry. I'm sorry, Darcy. But that's what he was doing to her. She's so small – she's like a little bird, and he was smashing her head into the stones, the wall.' He gasped for breath. 'He was breaking her.'

Awkwardly, I put an arm around him and he seemed glad of it. Behind him the morning zazen regulars stepped back, the friends he'd known in silence giving him privacy.

'When I got to her, her face was cut; her eye, it was swelling. Her hands – God, her hands, it was like they'd been shredded. I just held her. She was moaning. I can still hear her.'

'Did you call nine-one-one?'

'I didn't want to let go of her. I hated to. I had to . . . to get the phone.'

'That was the right thing to do.'

He nodded, disbelieving. 'Then I held her, told her it'd be all right, they were coming, they'd take care of her. She said something – something in her language, I don't know what. I pretended I did because I couldn't bear to make her explain.'

'Her language? Where is she from?'

'Maybe Thailand. Or a place near there. Or near Malaysia.'

So, somewhere in Southeast Asia.

Behind me, she moaned. I snapped around in time to see the paramedics shifting her onto the stretcher. Her head was braced like they do with the possibly broken necks of football players. And stunt doubles. People moved back to create a lane, and as the stretcher passed Tully reached out to touch her. The smell of antiseptics, of medical fluids, threw up a wall around her, as if she was already in the ER and we were locked out in the waiting room.

For an instant the hospital waiting room, not knowing if Leo would make it, was the reality. The gut-level fear.

Leo? Was he watching this from upstairs? From my window over the courtyard? Renzo supporting him so he didn't fall? I tried to see the window but it was too dark.

Sirens yelped. Coming nearer. More police cars – code three?

Tully started after the paramedics.

A cop – Snell! – stepped in front. 'We need some information.' And Tully stopped, nodding vaguely.

Undone as Tully was, the last thing he needed was a face-to-face with Snell. 'Tully,' I said, 'who did this to Lila?'

'That man! The one who follows her here. Looks like a hit man, an enforcer – short, big chest. You've seen him. From her work. Lila's terrified.'

'You know that? He's from her work? Employed there? Or a customer?'

'Yes.'

Whatever that meant.

Behind Tully, Snell was taking it all in but saying nothing. He looked almost as shaky as Tully. On the sidewalks a second, looser clutch of watchers eyed the ambulance. The morning zazen people who'd sat with him in the zendo but maybe never spoken to him as they all rushed off after the last bell toward offices or studios, stayed put.

'Tully, what did Lila say about him, her assailant?'

'Her English, you know, it's not much. I don't know how she manages her work. Guess that's not heavy on words.'

I nodded. Pole dancing and extras. Yes or no. Pay or not. 'But him?'

'I tried twice. She shrunk up. Turned away. Like she was afraid I asked. Like he might be watching her. Like he . . . what he did. Like he might beat the crap out of her!' His face flushed and his hand balled into fists, the kind that squeeze in on themselves.

I turned to Snell. 'I've seen him here. She always looked scared. Other people must have seen him. He looks like a bouncer, like pure muscle. She is, I think – I can't be sure – a pole dancer on Broadway.'

Tully nodded. 'I wanted to help her. I tried to tell her. I . . . couldn't.'

'We'll go to the hospital. I'll be with you there. Do you need to call your job?'

Suddenly there was an eruption of sirens. Two patrol cars slung round the corner. Another ambulance raced in behind.

They screeched to a halt in front of the zendo.

Before I could ask anything the paramedics were out of the van and racing toward us. 'Where?' one asked Snell. Snell shook his head.

'There's already been an ambulance here. It just left,' I said.

'They called us. Victim in the courtyard.'

Another—

I hurried into the courtyard. The far wall, the back of a building on Broadway, was two stories high. Nothing in front but two stone benches. Empty benches. I spun toward the low stone wall on this side, the street side, the place the homeless guy had slept last night. Nothing but two big ceramic planters.

Nothing till I looked down to the far corner. There, against the wall, like something thrown out of the way, lay the victim.

'Omigod! Renzo!'

FIFTEEN

People said things. The clutch of morning zazen sitters who had drunk Renzo's coffee other days, nibbled on the pastries he showed up with at the end of the sittings, now looked dazed. Nobody quite knew how they could have let Renzo lay unconscious yards away and not noticed.

Jeffrey Dedham: 'I was so caught up in the girl here.' *The girl.* Lila Suranaman was so incidental she didn't even have a name to a guy who'd probably been here every morning she had. Had that been her choice? Or her shyness, her terror?

'I was keeping an eye peeled for the police. They got here in eight minutes – I checked, but it seemed like eight years.' Hudson Poulsson looked even less focused than when he drove Leo home from San Francisco General.

'I was so worried.' Aurelia said just that. On the set she'd been clothed to attract eyes, not withstand cold. Now, an hour later, she was shaking. I couldn't guess how much was from shock and concern for a woman she'd never spoken to. Or if it was the aftermath of storming off the set. Frankly, I was shocked that she was here.

'I was looking for you or – oh, shit! – for Renzo.' Tully Lennox had to swallow hard before he could tell me that Renzo had come running from the cafe with him when they heard Lila screaming. He – Tully – had rushed to her, he said. Renzo had tackled her attacker. Renzo, the benevolent ruler of this little kingdom surrounding his cafe, had flung himself at the 'devil,' as someone had called the man.

I wasn't asking questions; I was standing behind the paramedics, too close, they kept telling me. I moved back for a moment. A thrust of fog-damp air caught me and for an instant cleared the chemical stench. I inched forward, desperate for a lane to see Renzo's eyelid flicker, to reach in and touch him, assure him I was here.

When the paramedics rolled his unmoving body out past the

stone wall, wheels clattering across the sidewalk, and into their van, we all, the morning zazen people, Roman Westcoff and even Officer Snell, watched, dazed. The courtyard resounded emptiness. I looked toward the zendo doors where Renzo had left me espressos the mornings before zazen, where we'd talked in hushed tones about Leo after his attack, where Renzo had made a point of greeting strangers on Saturday mornings. The whole place now seemed hollow and cold.

In the moments I stood there, the paramedics siren'd off, a crime-scene van pulled up, a plainclothes officer – detective, no doubt – and a woman and man in uniform hurried up to Snell. Suddenly the silence had turned inside out and everything was noise – radios spitting words, engines humming one over another, horns beeping and tires screeching on Columbus as traffic narrowed into two lanes. Fog was thinning, turning the scene a slightly less dreary gray and showing more clearly the grim lines on faces. With the detective firing questions, Snell seemed as stunned as the rest of us, as if he was sweeping words toward a scooper hoping to spot an answer. It was, I realized, Roman Westcoff who had been throwing out questions before. Now with a detective on site the reporter had eased back into the group of us. He was slipping his notebook into his jacket. The detective passed him without a glance.

'Are you the assistant abbot here?' the detective was asking me.

'Assistant *to* the abbot,' I corrected.

'To the abbot. And the abbot is—'

Leo! I pushed past the detective and ran for the zendo, up the stairs, and pulled open Leo's door.

Leo was standing, arms propped on the high ledge of his bedroom window overlooking the courtyard. The window was small, and with its height and the ledge that kept him a few inches back from the glass, he couldn't see the part of the courtyard near the building. Most times if he wanted to check on a noise or watch for an arrival he used the window in my room. This morning, he looked as if he had exhausted all his strength just to pull himself to standing. He looked like a peg holding up the gray sweatshirt and pants he slept in. He was staring, or maybe his eyes were just facing the window. He started to speak, cleared his throat, and said in a raspy voice, 'Tell me what happened.'

I did. 'But by the time I got here the attack was over.'

'The attacker?'

'Gone.'

'Who?'

I told him.

'Are they sure?'

'No one saw the attack, so that's the best guess. I doubt even Renzo could add more. Tully Lennox saw Renzo tackling him. But Tully was so caught up in Lila, he's not going to be a great witness. He's gone to the hospital with her. Do you want me to call—'

'No, no. How are they, Renzo, Lila?'

'I don't know.' As I spoke the words took on reality. 'I saw their limp bodies wheeled out of here with paramedics on both sides. Neither of them was moving, but I don't know what that signifies.'

'Not like football players holding up a fist.'

'Yeah, no rallying the troops. But that doesn't mean anything. Really. They'll be fine.'

'Pretty picture.'

Picture. Illusion; not reality. I swallowed hard. 'Leo, it's the best I can do. Renzo . . .' And then I lost it. And Leo, weak as he was, held me while I sobbed on his shoulder. 'Lila . . .' I said, stepping back. 'I knew she was frightened. 'The man . . . I saw him . . . once, twice. Maybe if I—'

'Maybe.'

I nodded. He was saying the same thing as 'pretty picture,' imaginary states I was creating to comfort myself in a situation where I didn't – couldn't – know what was real. Where I didn't want to see a bad picture, couldn't balance on the mushy footing of uncertainty. 'Not knowing is the highest,' someone said. I wouldn't have been surprised if he quoted that now. But his face looked no more composed than mine and I had the feeling that he too was balancing on ground that had suddenly lost its solidity.

I waited, desperate for him to return to being something I could hang onto. Even though, as he said, as Suzuki-roshi had said years ago, as I knew, *things change.*

In a moment, he said, 'Help me downstairs.' He didn't mention that yesterday it would have been Renzo who wrapped his arm around his back and eased him down the stairs.

'Leo, you don't have to—'

'I have to.'

'The police—'

'Not for them.'

'What did the doctor say? Has he been here to see you this morning?'

'No.'

'But—'

'Darcy! I know what I'm doing.'

I had the feeling he was reassuring himself. His eyes shifted in the way of one making a decision. I could have pressed him, but in this moment he seemed to me not a Zen master but a standard-issue stubborn man, like my dad, or one of my brothers who was going to lift this box or boulder and that was just that.

He was making an effort to walk steadily as we lurched down step after step. His body felt so insubstantial against my arm and shoulder, and the gamey smell of sickness came and went. In the hall he paused, his breath thick, nodding at the patrol officer who must have followed me when I ran in here. I gave silent thanks to SFPD for this consideration of waiting down here.

For a moment, I thought Leo would realize that he wasn't so much walking as draping himself over me. Then I was sure he would pull together every bit of strength, square his shoulders and walk out into the courtyard. What he did was make his way through the madrone doors with me helping him, just as he was. A few people half-gasped. The last time they'd seen him was before he was attacked, before the hospital, the days in bed. Only Hudson Poulsson had been with him when he looked worse than this. Even the detective tacitly acknowledged the situation. He waited while Leo spoke a few words to each of the morning zazen people, telling them he'd moved into the 'don't worry about' category, that Buddhism did not insulate us from life, au contraire, and ending by assuring them I was on the way to the hospital and I'd have news of Renzo and Lila this evening. Leo even caught Westcoff's eye and said, 'As long as you're going to be pestering her, drive her to the hospital.'

'No,' I snapped. 'Not necessary. Your car's not far.'

'Let him drive you.'

I nodded, appreciating Leo's concern, and hoping I wasn't

about to leave the safe frying pan of my own driving and leap into the fire with Westcoff. The reporter had none of that hesitation. His face brightened. He might as well have decorated his forehead with neon-flashing *captive interrogee.*

The detective passed me on to an assistant, suitable for a witness who had witnessed nothing. Westcoff kept his distance as if holding behind his back a box of chocolate clues he didn't want to share. Or maybe he had other, unrelated reasons for keeping distant from authority. Whatever, as soon as we cleared the courtyard he scurried behind the sidewalk onlookers and then angled back to his car. When he drove up he'd have had the whole curb at his command. Now, the little car was wedged between two patrol cars and flashers from a van sent odd patterns of light onto the windshield. Voices were shouting over each other like a word-ball fight.

I'd barely slid in and shut the door when he had the engine on and was demanding, 'So, what do you make of this?'

'Renzo?'

'Went to save the girl. Got waylaid?'

'It's so Renzo.' I sighed. 'Did you know him?'

'Of course.'

Of course. What kind of reporter would he have been to overlook a source like Renzo?

The car Westcoff was inching back and forth between patrol cars was a little green Fiat the color of Mom's Formica kitchen table. 'I pictured you driving something with balled tires and fenders from the junk yard.'

'So'd my ex.' He grunted, lugging the wheel all the way back left. 'She took the condo. Much as we owed, it's almost a straight deal. You know the assailant?'

Huh? It took me a moment to realize he'd switched topics without taking a new breath. The early morning was catching up with me. Ditto the lack of coffee. I yearned to rest my head against the window and let Westcoff jolt the car back and forth in silence. I said, 'You mean the guy who attacked Lila? The thug in the dark suit? I've seen him, or a close likeness of him, outside the zendo a couple times. Lila was scared.'

'Why didn't you—'

'Save her?' I snapped.

'A little defensive, assistant to the abbot?'

'Like you save everyone in danger! Save the baby or get the video?'

'I'm not a Buddhist.'

Yeah, right! I was way too tired to deal with this. 'Or a fair debater. Look, this is a constant issue for us. Homeless people sleep in the courtyard. Should we shoo them, call the police or let them in to sleep inside in the hall where it's warm?'

'Do the right thing?'

'There is no right thing! That's the point! What's right today isn't tomorrow. What should we have done for Lila – ask if the guy was following her? If he's dangerous? If she's sure? Demand she tell us in her iffy English? Tentative as she is, we'd probably never have seen her again.' I made myself stop and take a breath. 'It's not that we don't care. It's just not that easy.'

'That your abbot's philosophy?'

Did this guy never give up? 'Garson-roshi gives everyone the benefit of the doubt. He'd even talk to you.'

Westcoff laughed a little.

'When they bow, the Hindus mean, "I salute the divine within you." As a Buddhist, Leo really believes in giving people the chance to be . . .'

'Better than their crappy selves?'

I nodded and let it go, then watched as he made two more passes at the patrol car bumper ahead. If he'd had the kind of vehicle I'd pictured for him he could have rammed it over the bumper, but a shiny new possession is a burden. This one didn't even have a 'used' smell. There were no crumpled take-out bags, not so much as an old newspaper. When he cleared the hurdle and eased through the mess of vehicles and made it to the corner, I said, 'You've been digging around – do you know where Lila works?'

'Oh, yeah. The *Tink Pitty*. Get it, play on letters?'

'I live here; I've seen the sign.'

'It is to the old established strip clubs what strip clubs are to the symphony. Even their poles are dirty, not that the clientele cares.'

'Clientele?'

'Seedy old guys. Sleaze tourists.'

'Poor Lila.'

'Poor lots of girls. I've done a lot on trafficking – drugs and human—'

'Both?'

'They're not always separate. Look, drug smuggler spots a fresh face, gives her a little coke to carry on a plane back to the States. If she makes it through customs it's hers, and then it's a matter of time before she's his.'

'And if she's caught?'

'No trail to him. Business write off.' He shrugged. 'What I'm saying is you could have done more for this girl.'

'So could you!'

He swung the little coupe hard left, flinging me into the door. *Very mature!* I didn't say that. I took another long breath, rubbed my fingers against my jeans legs to shift my attention, then said, 'So, you made a big point of telling me you're the only one who cares about Leo's attack besides me. That was twenty-four hours ago. What you have discovered since?'

'The thug – why would he come at your abbot?'

'That's your discovery – a question? Great sleuthing.' It was still too dark to be sure but odds were his jaw tightened and there might have been a little flush across embarrassed cheeks. 'What makes you think – assume – the thug today is the same guy?'

'Two attacks, same place, less than a week,' he said, pulling into the next lane in front of a truck. 'At the site of the pimp fight six weeks ago.'

The pimp fight! So that's how our Zen Center came to Westcoff's notice. But I didn't let myself get sidetracked.

Westcoff was hunched over the wheel as if he was in a bumper car park. Unlike Hudson Poulsson, three days ago, Westcoff was taking a maze of city streets, weaving left when he could, going against rush hour traffic. I had my feet braced on the floorboards. 'Why,' he said, doing a quick right–left check, 'would the thug attack your abbot? Let's assume he did. Assume he had a reason.'

'Maybe he resented Lila having a safe place to go.'

'And the abbot for offering it to her?'

'Leo didn't offer it directly to her. It's not like we sent flyers. Not like our sittings are at convenient times—'

'They were for her.'

'Coincidence.'

'But close enough in his mind.'

Point taken. 'I don't think,' I said more slowly, 'that she ever spoke to Leo. She drank coffee at Renzo's— Omigod, do you think he was really after Renzo? That's Lila wasn't the target at all?'

Westcoff shot onto Van Ness Avenue, inches behind the bumper of a truck. At the corner he swung right, then left. I stopped looking. I felt like the thug's motives were bouncing around in the car and I couldn't grab hold of them as we swayed from corner to corner.

'Suppose,' Westcoff said, 'our thug was set on putting fear into Renzo. Suppose he grabbed Lila to lead him to Renzo—'

'He wouldn't need her for that. Everybody knows where Renzo is. The thug could have walked into the cafe any time after seven a.m. He could have waited till Renzo closed up at night.'

'OK, suppose . . . suppose . . . it was spur of the moment.'

'OK. But it's Lila he attacked. People saw him attacking her and then Renzo running to help her. Because she screamed.' I held up a hand, not that he was in a position to see. 'When she screamed, Renzo and Tully were in the cafe. So he wasn't after them. He attacked Lila, because . . . because he was jealous, or . . . he figured he owned her, or . . . she owed him. Whatever.'

'But—'

'Maybe he resented having such a lousy job. Rotten hours, miserable pay. Sometimes a grudge is all a guy's got and he's not about to let go, because, Westcoff, it's all he's got.' His Buddha. *If you meet the Buddha in the road . . .* But I definitely was not going into that analogy with Westcoff.

I'd had the safety discussion with Leo, more restrainedly, questioning how far we trust before we take measures, but I sure wasn't going to bring that up with Westcoff. I might as well wade in with John. 'You still haven't mentioned a single thing you've uncovered. Or have you been spending your days at the beach?' I sat back against the righteousness of my position and waited.

'There's got to be a connection,' he said, as much to himself as to me.

'No, there doesn't. But it'd make a much bigger story,

right?' I almost felt bad when I said it. In the clearer light of morning I could see that this time I had pierced him. 'Westcoff, just why is this such a big deal for you?'

'Hey, I'm a journalist.'

'But why *this* story?'

A U-drive van veered out from the cross street. I braced. Westcoff shot left. He pulled back into his lane, but the whole maneuver reminded me how much I hated driving with amateurs. As for him, I had the feeling he was using my relieved silence as a shield. He was nearly to SF General when he said, 'I'm a journalist. When I was a kid I dreamed of being a reporter, breaking the big stories, beating out the competition, ripping the cover off graft, corruption and the world of evil. When I got hired by the *Chronicle*, I was in heaven. You want to know why?'

'Why?'

'Because your local paper is where stories get dug up.' He looked momentarily abashed, like either he'd exposed too much or he just wanted to edit that last statement. 'Before a story goes national, it's a local reporter who spots it, who digs, and who keeps digging. We're the ones who know the players, the angles, the history, the city. Our city.'

'But?'

'Financially we're on the edge all the time. By the time we run a national story it's all over the Web. You remember: Breaking! Breaking! Read all about it! Extra! Well that's not possible any more in a local paper. Plus ad revenue is in the toilet. Everything's tight. And . . .'

I finished for him. 'It's reporters who get laid off.'

'Yeah, with nowhere to go. You survive by spotting stories before anyone else, having better sources, by knowing your city.' He pulled up by a loading zone, got out and shut the door carefully.

He was halfway to the Emergency entrance when I caught up. 'OK, show me how a reporter gets information . . . about Renzo. Get me more than the standard "Wait."'

'In surgery,' he said ten minutes later, 'you're going to be here a while. Waiting.' Fingers to forehead, he gave me a salute and almost made it to the door before circling back. 'Call me,' he said more hesitantly. 'I'll come drive you home.'

I smiled. 'Won't be necessary. When word gets out that Renzo's in Emergency, this place will standing room only. I'll have six offers of rides from my family alone.'

'Call me anyway.'

'Business or concern?'

'Both.' He started toward the doors again.

'Hey, Westcoff, you still haven't told me one thing you learned since Leo's attack.'

His brown eyes sashayed back and forth. He might as well have been doing the Truth or Lie Two-step. Which would he choose? I decided, as Leo would, to give him the benefit of the doubt.

'You cannot repeat this.'

'Good opener.' Did the man really have something? Something he would not have told me if I hadn't badgered him three times?

'A third grader could break into your abbot's car.'

'You broke into Leo's car!'

'Hey, don't look like I stole his mother's ashes. It's just a car.'

'Like his wallet, his toothbrush. *His!*'

'Hey, I thought you Buddhists were against attachment.'

'We're against— Oh, skip it. So, what you're saying is you've been on this for three days and all you've done is commit a petty crime?'

'Yeah, probably. Almost certainly. I checked the car out. Papers in the back, just Buddhist stuff. And then I went through the glove box.'

'And?'

'He has a Fastrak.'

'That's it? You broke into Leo's car and found that he has the same gadget as nearly every other driver in California?'

'I already knew he had a Fastrak. He used it twice on the Golden Gate last month, and on the Bay Bridge before that.'

'You broke into his car to check on the Fastrak you already knew he had? This is what journalism has sunk to?'

'It's what journalism has deduced. What were those trips?'

'Golden Gate? He gave a lecture at Green Gulch once. The other time we went to Point Reyes. The Bay Bridge trips I don't know—'

'Let me enlighten you then. You Buddhists like to be enlightened, right?'

The man was driving me crazy.

'One trip every month. Last Wednesday. Mean anything now?'

'No. But—'

'Don't bother. Here's what a journalist does, one with honed hunches and good sources and a few favors to call in.'

'Like your Fastrak source?'

'Nah, for that I just used the info in the glove box. Lesson: the glove box is not a safe deposit box. Don't put all your papers there. On the computer I am now Leo Garson of Pacific Avenue. As such I can track my record. If I had crossed the Bay Bridge or the Golden Gate every Wednesday I would know it. But I – Leo Garson, who normally uses his Fastrak, and who travels somewhere every fourth Wednesday, does not use it.'

'So?'

'So, why not?' *Moron!* But he didn't say that aloud.

'Maybe he took the BART train, or the bus. Maybe he drove with a friend. What's your point?'

'Where did he go?'

I turned to him, waited till I had his full attention. 'Answer me one question.'

'OK.'

'How come you're so caught up in this? No, wait. A Zen master is assaulted, but not fatally injured. By the next day, you're there. Why? You don't know Leo. You're not interested in Zen. Maybe this will turn out to be a big story for you, but, Westcoff, what made you think so?'

He hesitated.

'Don't answer me this and I will never tell you another thing.'

'OK, OK. This city is in the thick of trafficking. Leo Garson's the kingpin.'

SIXTEEN

eo, a kingpin! 'Yeah, right. He's also a race car driver and sings with The Dandy Warhols.'

Westcoff was in my face, here in the San Francisco General Hospital Emergency Department waiting room. Behind him, weary folk of both sexes and various ages sat up on their chairs. The whole thing was like a replay of three days ago when Leo was in surgery and his assailant came wheeling through into the hospital innards then went poof. I was not about to give ground. I leaned forward and said the only reasonable thing. 'Fuck off!'

'Is that how you Zen people—'

'This one, yeah.'

'Why don't you just ask your roshi? Ask him about the trafficking in your neighborhood. What does he know? Then ask him how he knows it. Ask him about the routes through the "respectable" strip joints along Broadway. Ask him—'

I laughed. 'Here's what's going on. You tell me where I'm wrong. You're digging for a story on trafficking. You heard about the pimp fight in our courtyard six weeks ago and you're salivating at the idea of involving a Zen priest. It'd be a break-out story for you. But you're not getting anywhere. Because, Westcoff, there is no connection. The cops arrested the pimps. You know zip about Leo, and maybe you've tried talking to him – you can believe I'll ask him that – but now you want me to excavate what he knows and bring it back to you.'

'I know he knows . . .'

'What?'

'He's involved.'

'You know that because?'

'I've got sources. I can't reveal them.'

'Sure. Call me when you've got something more than hope.'

The outside doors flew open. A gurney with pole, plastic bag and three paramedics swept in, a buzz of comments all around.

It had nothing to do with me, but now, in here, it seemed like all crises scraped off the outer layers of us all. When the far doors banged shut, silence settled back, as if the medical team had dragged that bit of life with them, leaving all of us to sink back into the miasma of waiting.

All except Westcoff, who was gone.

Time stretches in the tension-laced boredom of the waiting room. Each check of your watch signals a longer time spent in surgery, required for a condition more serious with a prognosis more dire. All of which are just thoughts, I reminded myself, as Leo would remind me. Thoughts masquerading as facts, just as Westcoff had dressed his suspicions as truth.

Within an hour, every one of Renzo's relatives had arrived and settled in clumps. Apparently not all of them cared for all the others. His friends – the people he called when he needed eyes-only information about public works or public housing, the opera, the bridge barrier – filtered in. A couple in pastel shorts and sweaters, tourists from Arkansas whom he'd guided to the Legion of Honor exhibit after giving them breakfast, announced they were praying for him, and a woman who might have been one of his aunts thanked them.

I started toward her, then reconsidered. Choosing the wrong team in a family standoff can mark you for life. Instead I moved to the middle of the room. 'I wonder,' I said in a loud voice, 'about Lila, the woman Renzo was trying to protect. Do we know how she's doing?'

'The doctor can find out when he comes to tell us about Renzo,' a short woman in a blue dress said.

Skepticism must have been clear on my face.

The woman patted my arm. 'Trust me, honey.'

More people arrived. At some point food appeared in hampers. Guards complained ineffectively. Before or after that I sat on the floor, leaned against the wall and fell asleep. I had the feeling the family was prepared to take over the halls and camp out in Renzo's room as soon as they could get him one.

Still, it was three in the afternoon before a weary woman in scrubs stepped through the door and asked for Mr Renzo's wife.

The doctor thought Renzo was his last name?

'Renzo has a wife!'

'My brother,' a plump, dark-haired woman shook her head, 'is married to that cafe of his.'

'He's under sedation. His shoulder was torn quite badly,' the doctor, a short woman with olive skin and pale green eyes announced in a slightly British accent. 'Ligaments torn from the bone. Two cracked ribs. Ulna fractured in two places. Metal plates. Pins.'

'Which arm?' a woman demanded.

'Will they stay in Uncle Renzo, or come out?'

'Rehab?'

The doctor seemed stunned. A man repeated, 'Which arm?'

'Left.'

Sighs came from all directions.

'Nothing else? Organ damage?'

I gave up searching for the source of the questions. The doctor seemed to, too.

'Nothing serious.'

Someone demanded just what that meant. Someone else hushed him. The doctor soldiered on, moving into the mushy area of prediction. 'No reason not to regain full control . . . Take some time.' And more firmly, 'Still sedated.' Most firmly, 'Two visitors max.'

'Lila?' I called out as the doctor turned away.

The woman in the blue dress materialized at her side. 'Lila Suranaman,' she said in the tone of one who had insisted two or three times before.

'Suranaman.' The doctor massaged the syllables. 'I will check.'

The woman in blue put a hand near but not on her scrub-covered shoulder. 'You can call, right?'

'No.' She whipped through the doors and was gone.

I doubted we'd see her again.

Right I was. A sturdy, dark-haired man who could have been a wrestler or a bouncer but must have been an intern appeared ten minutes later. 'Lila Suranaman,' he said, 'is no longer a patient here.'

'What?'

'She checked herself out an hour ago.'

This sure was one easy institution to leave.

Questions were shot at him. But it became clear he'd been fronted up not due to knowledge of Lila's condition but the lack of it.

Bad shape as she was in, she had to be desperate to even think of leaving the hospital. In here she'd been cared for and safe; on the street she was neither. She was a sitting duck for the guy who'd sent her here. If someone didn't find her, help her, she was going to end up dead.

I checked my messages. Leo texted that he had decided to cancel tonight's zazen. I was more relieved than I would have expected. Probably everyone was. How could they sit facing the wall, watching their breath while wondering if every creak or rattle signaled a new attack?

I thanked the woman in blue and got her promise she'd alert me to the smallest change in Renzo's condition.

Then I did the last thing I wanted to do. I called Westcoff.

SEVENTEEN

'd seen the Tink Pitty before but apparently I'd put it out of my mind. In the world of strip and sleaze it was seeping toward the bottom. At least for San Francisco, where strip clubs like Carol Doda's Condor have become close to historical landmarks and kids from the valley come for a night of pretend bad. They could, of course, count on real pole dancing and real, if speedy, lap-dancing and real fleecing.

Westcoff had eyed the *Parking $10* sign near the club and laughed. 'Ten bucks, that's the surcharge, on top of the regular twenty-five. They don't mention that till you pull in. Welcome to Broadway.' Four blocks farther on he stuffed his Fiat next to a tiny bit of curb. The man had answered my call so fast I'd barely had time to pop in to check on Leo, to let him know that Renzo would mend and I was headed off to find Lila Suranaman. 'With Westcoff.'

Leo had raised an eyebrow. He was good at that.

''S what you get for insisting I ride to the hospital with him.'

He nodded. 'Karma.'

Meaning, actions have consequences.

I'd been tempted to call one of my brothers to stay with him. Gary? Not unless I could drop Leo in his law office, and Leo'd be willing to read over depositions. John? I'd hesitated and ended up saying to Leo, 'Likely, I'll be late. Will you be OK?'

'I'm fine. Much better. I've been downstairs – don't look so shocked. Be pleased. Now, go, before you let that reporter up here.'

'He thinks you're a drug and trafficking kingpin.'

I expected Leo to laugh, to say something like: *Then we'd have padded zafus*. But he just shook his head as if to say that was too serious an issue to be taken that lightly.

Now dusk was turning dark as Westcoff and I strode the four uphill blocks from the shiny new buildings of the tech wave, past construction to defunct and graffiti'd strip joints of yore, to Indian and Chinese restaurants mixed in with the faux exotic and those clubs not yet on life support – the life cycle of Broadway in four blocks. Westcoff's hands were stuffed hard into the pockets of his tweed jacket as if to demonstrate just how he'd gone about ruining it. His head was thrust forward and he was panting, trying to match my pace. 'Hey, slow down there, Lott. I just brought you for the muscle.'

I kept up the pace another half block. *Take that for bad-mouthing Leo!*

As if intuiting my thoughts, he said, 'Tink Pitty's right behind your Zen place.'

'Not right behind. No one's going to be tunneling in for evening zazen.'

'Broadway backs Pacific. That's close as you can get.'

'Close in walking distance as any place within four blocks.'

'Still.'

'When you start with a conclusion and work the facts to fit, that's called fiction.'

Westcoff flinched, but just slightly, and we walked on in irritable silence; him trying to conceal his chugging breaths, me taking long strides up the hill, partly in reaction to too much sitting all day, mostly for spite. I was still wearing the black jeans, T-shirt and zip jacket I'd grabbed at four something this morning and trying to ignore greasy strands of unwashed hair that had slithered loose from the knot to snap at my face.

He was wrong about Leo, of course. But had Leo and I been wrong about Lila? *The way is not difficult for those without preferences*, China's Third Patriarch, Jianzhi Sengcan, taught. *The way is not difficult except for picking and choosing.* I understood that and yet . . .

If I asked Westcoff, he'd be delighted to point out that every minute of the day was picking and choosing, opting for, declining, yearning for, running away from. Asking Lila if she needed help, waiting for a better time. We hadn't been careless, we'd tried not to freak her. We'd—

The words fell out of my mouth. 'How do you know you've done the wrong thing when everything told you it was right?'

Westcoff said, 'Huh?'

'Nothing.' *I'll ask Leo.*

Leo, who had once been sure he was doing the right thing, and was wrong.

The Tink Pitty's neon sign, the pendulous peninsula of breast with the flashing red nipple, beckoned from an alley. We stopped and, like a tourist couple, stared.

'Omigod. Westcoff, look!' There, at the entrance, by a propped-open standard metal alley door, stood the guy who beat up Lila. Above him the bulbous breast's flashing nipple extended out into the alley, so that the red bulb doubled as a suggestion of a brothel. The whole arrangement hung inside a frame made of metal bars about a foot above the creep's head. The guy was short and thick, like a brick in a jacket. The flashing red light seemed to bounce off his black eye – a souvenir from this morning, surely. The end of his nose had been scraped and was crusted, and a bandage covered a good portion of his left cheek. 'I can't believe he's here at work like nothing happened. Haven't the cops—?'

'Who'd give them a description? Not Lila. Not you; you didn't see him. Not Renzo.'

'Still—'

'You know how to define "low priority?"'

Two couples, in jeans, T-shirts and thin Low Hog jackets they'd gotten at a cut-rate place in some warmer clime were conferring in a huddle near the door. I started toward them.

Westcoff grabbed my arm. 'Hey, this isn't like calling the hospital information desk. You got a plan?'

'Of course,' I lied. Play it by ear, that was my plan.

I skirted the tourists, faced the bouncer and forced a smile. 'I'm looking for Lila.'

He shrugged me off. Not a word.

'Tell me where she is and I'll leave.'

'Leave.' It came out as a grunt, like he'd practiced that in the mirror. His face was square and bare, his features lumpy even without the bruises and patches.

'Not without Lila.'

He stepped toward me, his breath awful and sweat not smelling so good. He glared at Westcoff. 'Get her outta here.'

The Low Hog quartet had vanished. It was just us three.

I sighed, shrunk and slinked off.

'What was that?' Westcoff's face had turned to angry blotches.

'Come on!' I took his arm. 'When I turn, drop your keys. Make noise.'

'What?' But softly.

'Now.' I started back toward the door. Westcoff's keys hit the pavement. The bouncer glanced down. I leapt, grabbed the bar at the bottom of the boob sign and swung my heels into his nose.

I heard the crack before his yelp. I leapt down beside him. 'Where is she?'

'Fuff you, bith!'

'Dammit, where is she?' Dammit, where was Westcoff?

'What the hell? Sendar?' A man, taller and thinner, appeared in the doorway.

'His nose may be broken,' I said. 'It looks awful. We can drive him to the hospital.'

Taller-thinner was considering when Sendar growled, 'No,' pushed himself up, eyed me, shoved Taller-thinner aside and vanished into the building.

Taller-thinner eyed first me and then Westcoff, considered again and said, 'You paid yet?'

'No.'

'No?' he shook his head. 'No? Fifteen years and no one ever gave me that answer. *No?* Hell, go on in.'

He was still shaking his head as we followed him inside.

'Don't lose sight of the door,' Westcoff whispered.

He had described the Tink Pitty as seedy. Right he was. The paint was, of course, pink. Or it had been before years of smoke, dirt and rubbings, the source of which I chose not to consider. And the air – it was like airplane air re-circulated twice daily between SFO and Mars. The main surprise in the main room was the step down into the dark. I just caught myself in time and Westcoff smacked into me. The sole, dim light was a spot on a girl dancing, drugged but from her expression not nearly enough. Even as the thought struck me it seemed ridiculously obvious, still I wondered how she – how Lila – could stand doing this night after night. Points to Lila for not being drugged out of her mind.

I knew I'd only seen the vestibule of awful. As my eyes adjusted, three forms at two tables took shape – a man at the far table, and nearer, a hetero couple, their faces lit by a faux candle.

She was grinning; he was not. She was whispering, he not. Come morning she'd be telling friends every detail of this foray; he would not.

The bartender was staring at us.

Westcoff whispered, 'Outside.' When we cleared the door into the alley he grabbed my arm and hurried me toward the street. 'No one in there can give us anything.'

'Can or will?'

'Right. That dancer wouldn't remember Lila if she shared a room with her.'

We were on Broadway. I stopped. He was still pulling on my arm. 'Hey, I'm not a dog! We can't just abandon Lila. Let her be shipped off to the next brothel or stuffed in a basement and left to die.'

'Come on.'

'I'm serious.'

'As am I, Darcy Lott.' He lowered his voice. 'Not here. Trust me.'

I balanced the options. Trusting him was better than nothing. He picked up pace and slipped around the corner onto Columbus and chin-motioned toward a space between buildings. It was about two feet wide, carpeted with weeds and rubble. And dead dark. I couldn't see how far back it went. 'Emergency exit from a number of Broadway operations.'

'Really? I've walked this block hundreds of times.' Renzo's Caffe was at the corner. 'I never gave this . . . thing . . . a thought. I guess a person could squeeze through – not a fat person – but it'd have to be an emergency all right.'

'Plenty of those.'

'I'd think the cops would station themselves here like ants by a termite hole. I'd think the strip staff would know that.'

'Sometimes. But the cops are smart. They give the pimps and enforcers time to forget. The girls, they come and go, shipped in from Asia, shipped out to Vegas. Most don't even know about this. The other end's even less inviting. Rat Alley. That's what the old hands call this.'

'Sendar? Is he an old rat?'

'Old enough. I've seen him use this alley more than once. If we wait, we can follow him right back to his nest.'

'As opposed to?'

'We go out for sushi and he walks free.'

So we stood silently, peering into the alleyway while trying not to look like we were doing just that. An ambulance sped down Columbus, op-op-op-ing its way to collect someone for the most terrifying ride of their life. A bus chugged along, windows lit like an Edward Hopper painting, the passengers – only two – looking downward, probably at their phones.

Westcoff grabbed my arm. 'Oh, shit!'

'What?'

'There's another rat hole. I forgot about that. Shit! One they've used when this one's, you know, not serviceable.'

'When the cops are watching this one?'

'Right.'

'That one's worse than this trail of weed and garbage?'

He shrugged. 'It's trickier. Goes through a couple of basements that can be . . . bad. Trust me.'

'Life's hard for the fleeing bouncer.'

Westcoff let that ride and I said, 'So, now what? We wait and hope?'

'Let me check the other exit. It comes out by a store on the next block, but the place was boarded up last time I went by. Sendar could get there if he's desperate—'

'Why would he be desperate?'

'But he might have to climb rubble to get to the street. Let me check.'

'Now?'

'Don't worry. We've got time. He's going to be half an hour to deal with his nose alone. You really did a number on that. It's probably broken. Do you Zen—'

'Stunt doubles take no shit.'

'Say another quarter hour to decide if he's going to stay on the job, which he won't, believe me.'

'So, you know him.'

'Know enough.'

'But not where he lives?'

'Bad guys travel light. We could check his last-known address but then we wouldn't be here. If we're wrong, we're screwed.'

'You been on this story a long time?'

'Yeah,' he said in a weary tone. 'Long enough to see the end of the tunnel . . . blocked. A couple times. You think the rings are busted and they pop up again. New name, new location. New mules, new girls. Some from Malaysia, some from Milwaukee, Fresno, Tuscaloosa. Depressing.'

'OK. How long'll you be gone?'

'Five minutes. Ten outside.'

What could I say? 'Go. Fast!'

He made tracks for Broadway and turned the corner north.

I stepped back into a recessed doorway three feet beside the alley. I could handle this better on my own anyway. Columbus Avenue was busy enough to prevent a man from attacking a woman with no one calling 911. If Sendar used the alleyway, he would pop out onto the sidewalk before I saw him, but then he'd be on the sidewalk and have to turn around to see me. And he was the only one of us who'd be surprised.

It's cold in San Francisco at any time of year. Any night. This night. There are Tibetan exercises I've heard of in which you concentrate and warm your body. If I'd learned them I'd have been warmer. As it was I clutched my arms across my chest and waited, listening to the traffic, the wind shovel leaves along the pavement, radios blare and subside. If it were morning I'd be smelling the aroma of Renzo's coffee, the special morning bun with cinnamon and just a hint of grapefruit jelly threaded through. I'd tested a few that dazzled me but Renzo deemed imperfect.

Renzo. I wanted to check my phone for an update but didn't dare.

What was happening here? Leo, Lila, Renzo? I didn't have words, just felt the hollowness of grief. I'd been so shocked, so frightened for Leo, and now his injury seemed minor in comparison, his danger passed, his attack an aberration that had come and was gone. Compared to Lila.

Lila. I didn't know what her injuries were. In a way they were beside the point. The attack was the point. Was that the standard pimp slapping his women back in line? Had Lila checked herself out of the hospital and gone back to that life?

Or just gone?

Had she checked herself out or been taken out?

Or was she involved in something I had no idea about? Not

taking refuge in our zendo but meeting someone there? Smuggling? Something else?

Footsteps were slapping the sidewalk. Not running, but fast. Leather. Not quiet.

I pressed back into the dark of the doorway and waited, ready for Westcoff being careless, ready for a stranger making tracks on this deserted block.

I was not ready to hear heavy footsteps coming down the alleyway.

EIGHTEEN

Something moved in the narrow space between the buildings. Coming closer. Slowly. Shoes catching in underbrush? It would have been so much easier for anyone from the Tink Pitty to walk out the door beneath the neon breast into their own paved alley and onto Broadway. This route – overgrown, narrow, home to vermin – a person had to have a very good reason to choose it. It was a hiking boot route and the Tink Pitty people were the buffed dress shoes and spike heel set.

A hand slapped one of the brick walls. A stumble? In another couple seconds he – Sendar? – would be on the sidewalk.

I shrank back against the shop door. The recessed entry blocked light but it sucked in paper bags, foil-lined bags, plastic cups. I shifted. It sounded like I was wearing ankle bells.

Where the hell was Westcoff? Did he find someone at the other exit and go off after them?

The footsteps stopped. Was Sendar or whoever still in the weeds? Poking his head out? Looking up the sidewalk past me?

Paper rattled on the sidewalk. A can clattered. A motorcycle shot down Columbus, grinding over everything.

I strained to hear Sendar moving. Pants, jacket – something was fluttering in the wind.

A bus grumbled down the far side of Columbus.

A figure on the sidewalk shot past me.

Small. Hair caught inside her coat. A woman, surely. I just stopped myself before letting out a huge sigh. Lila Suranaman? Was it? I couldn't be sure. She was half-walking, half-running, lurching uphill toward Broadway, toward the strip clubs, toward traffic, the crowds, safety maybe? Toward buses, cabs? Was she limping? Her hat covering not just her hair but her bandages?

Bad as her injuries were, how could she manage this? How desperate was she?

I started forward. My foot caught on a tangle of garbage. *Shit!* I bent to free it.

A man ran awkwardly up the sidewalk right past me.

Sendar! It was really him! I recognized his walk.

Lila wouldn't know he was on her tail.

Yanking strands of who-knows-what off my ankles, I hurried after him. Sendar was moving like a freight train with an unbalanced load, making himself easy to tail on this dark, empty block. The man had his own injuries. Still, I kept my distance.

When I reached the corner at Broadway, the world shifted – light glowed, colors clashed, horns screamed, radios shot out discordance, voices grumbled, yelled, whooped. A bottle shattered at my feet. A car squealed a U-turn. Brakes screeched. 'Asshole!' 'Fuck you!'

The traffic light changed. Green to cross Broadway. Cars in the left-hand lane bumper-to-bumper'd onto Columbus against the light. Horns blew. I almost missed seeing Lila Suranaman, a white bandage on her face shining in the light, walking with obvious pain across the street, trying to hide among groups of celebrants. A truck shot around my corner. A man in a Giants jacket leapt back on the curb, too shocked to shake his fist till the truck was half a block away. A van turned slowly, inching through pedestrians. I scanned again to pick out Lila. I wanted to see which route she chose before I made my move. North into the crowds in North Beach? East along the far side of Broadway past the bigger, better strip clubs? Into Chinatown and maybe the police station. If she—

My head smacked into the pavement. Fireworks of white light shot around my eyes. Sounds hardened into a solid mass. Time stopped. I didn't know where I was. I rolled, banged into something. Noises now. A yelp. Words. ''Kay?' 'She!' 'Are you OK?'

Colors shifted to forms. Legs. People bending. I tried to push myself up. A hand pressed me back down.

'Don't move.'

'You shouldn't move an injured person, right, Eddie?'

'Wait. Should I call nine-one-one?'

I gave my head a shake, took hold of the nearest arm, stood and forced out, 'No.'

'Are you sure you—'

'I'll be OK. Thank you. All of you, thank you.' I didn't need them to tell me what happened – I could figure it out – but I asked, 'Did you see the man who hit me?'

'Someone hit you? Are you sure?'

'Yeah, some thug, but I didn't see his face.'

'Never mind,' I said. 'Which way did he go?'

'You're not going after him, are you?' A woman grabbed my arm.

'Not unless he's moving very slowly. I just need to know where he went.'

'That way.'

'No, over there, into Chinatown.'

'No.'

'Never mind. But thanks, really.' My head throbbed. My knees were jelly.

'You should make a police report.'

'When I get home. I only live a block away.'

'Are you—'

'I'll be fine, really. Thanks.'

I'd be marginal. Likely look worse. I took a deep breath to steady myself and walked, very carefully, as if I was doing the white line after three martinis, down the sidewalk I'd come on. I had the sense the well-wishers were watching me but very glad not to be any more involved.

In ten steps the scene switched back from color to black and white, from bursts of noise to memories of it, from the crush of traffic to spikes of single cars. To me alone and wobbly.

Feel your feet on the ground. This step. This step. Stay in what's real. Keep walking. The air was cold and moist – it snapped my hair against my sore face. But the cold felt good on my cheeks. My face was going to bruise. *Faster, go faster.* If my sisters and brothers spotted bruises I'd hear about it and keep hearing. And Mom! Mom would be planted in the hall between Leo's and my rooms when I woke up.

Feel your feet on the ground! I did, but they didn't feel like appendages adjusting for balance. They felt rounded on the sides, almost numb, and the toes I couldn't sense at all.

The stunts! Oh, shit, the stunts! My whole career hung on those stunts. How was I ever going to balance on the dolly well enough to handle the Lombard curves? No way could I—

Bruises! I couldn't show up on the set with a black eye or a purple face, not me, the one who was fighting to change the gag set-up. *Oh, sure, believe the new girl who can't even stay on her feet.*

Arnica! I could smear it all over my face, my elbows; it'd stop the bruising. If I rubbed it on soon. Very soon . . .

Faster! Go faster!

I rounded the corner by Renzo's dark cafe and started down the sidewalk to the courtyard. Less than an hour ago I'd been thinking how many attack victims we'd had here. Now I was one of them. Sort of.

Pacific was darker than Columbus and emptier. Cars were bumper to bumper along the curbs, gratefully abandoned by tourists now drooling in the strip joints a block away. Dark cars. Empty sidewalks. Noise all behind me. Only the rasp of the wind here and the smack of my feet hitting the sidewalk, louder, clearer with each step. I was treading heavily, trying to slap life back into the soles, trying to keep my balance and not slow my pace. I glued my eyes to the zendo doors as if they'd grow branches to tow me in. When I came abreast the stone courtyard wall it was like finding a friend. I was tempted to run a hand along the familiar rough top. I didn't. Eyes on the doors, I kept moving.

When I rounded the edge into the courtyard, I let out a sigh.

Hands grabbed me from behind.

Instinctively I elbowed back, slammed down my foot. Stomped an instep? I pulled free and spun round.

Sendar! How did he—

He grabbed me around the ribs and jammed his elbows in. I could barely breathe. He rammed his knees into my legs from behind, bracing to throw me down. I kicked hard at his shin bone.

He yelped. His arms went slack. I jumped away. His arm came up, thick, black-coated, back-handed across my face. I stumbled. I could feel myself falling.

Suddenly, he wasn't hitting me.

He'd stopped.

I stumbled back against the wall.

He was still there.

Fighting someone else.

Someone had him in a head hold.

I blinked again and again, trying to make out the action through my half-swollen eyes in the dark. Clothes flapped, arms flew. Grunts, screams. Hair flying.

A woman yelled. He was fighting a woman!

I pushed to get up, to help, but my legs went flaccid.

The woman was slamming a bag into his face. Eye gouging. He screamed. They were moving fast around each other, dark clothes against dark clothes.

She had him by the hair. Her own hair was bouncing.

I shoved myself up.

Fell back against the wall.

Sirens sounded in the distance. There weren't coming here; I didn't fool myself.

Sendar was on his feet, facing the woman. He was feeling in his pocket for something. To hit with? To shoot with?

I had to do something.

I pushed hard to get up. And fell back.

The siren whirled down and stopped. Somewhere. Not here.

'Nine-one-one?' I said, loudly. 'A man, Sendar, is attacking a woman. Pacific Avenue just east of Columbus. You'll be—'

He turned and stared at me, at my empty hand. In the dark. Again, the siren rose. In a second he was out of the courtyard and gone.

The woman was in the shadows, bent over, panting.

'You OK?' I got out. My lips were swelling.

'Better . . . than you.'

'Pretty low standard.'

She moved toward me, out of the dark.

'You certainly have unexpected talents,' I said.

NINETEEN

'Maybe stunt work is for you, Aurelia. Fight scenes, anyway, if you can learn to pull your punches.'

'Can't promise that.'

'You're a real street fighter. How'd you learn that?'

'Camp.' She was bending over me, eyeing my face. 'You need the Emergency Room.'

'Not a chance. You couldn't get me back there if I was dead.'

I thought for a moment she'd have another try about the ER, but she just smiled.

'I've had worse falls,' I said. 'This one'll leave me blossoming ugly colors, but I don't think anything's broken. Can you help me upstairs?'

'Do you need any—'

'Between my sister, the doctor, and tips from other stunt doubles on the sets, I'm prepared. If it exists, I've got it.'

'OK, let's see whacha got!'

For a small person she was strong, much more so than I'd have guessed, and I'd seen her in a T-shirt that wasn't cut to hide anything. By the time we'd made it to the doors I was feeling better, but maneuvering the stairs was no cake walk.

Leo's door was shut. If a fight in the courtyard hadn't woken him, our footsteps probably wouldn't either. Still, I tiptoed across the landing.

The bathroom is cramped for one person. But I felt shaky enough to be glad Aurelia was there as I plucked tubes from the medicine cabinet and poured pills from bottles. I held out the Arnica for her. 'You look like maybe you got a little too much sun, maybe cut yourself shaving.'

She laughed. 'I get clumsy with that beard.'

'Spread it thin, it's homeopathic. Less is more. Face, muscles, wherever you need it. Though you were giving more than getting in that fight.'

'That's one asshole who's going to think twice about bruising another woman.'

I nodded, then had a good look in the mirror. My eyes were already sporting purple underneath. One cheek was red and my nose looked as if it had been scraped with a file. 'Shit! Shit, shit, shit!'

'You'll be OK. A little makeup—'

'A vat! But yeah. Actually, it's not my face as much as my butt muscles, my legs.'

'You're thinking of the stunt, huh?'

'Yeah. Sorry, just whining out loud.'

She hesitated.

I read her thoughts like a large print book. In a vaguely similar situation years ago I'd had those same thoughts, and stood like Aurelia Abernathy was now, trying to figure out a tactful way to say it. 'Yeah, Aurelia, if I can't do the stunt come Monday morning I'll put in a good word for you.'

'Wow. Terrific. I really need a job. My . . . guy is pressing me. I was on the verge of hitting up – taking barista training.'

Her guy was pressing her? I didn't want to know. Not tonight. 'Hey, this isn't definite. I'll probably be fine by Monday, or close enough. This gag is a big deal for me; I'm not going to blow it off.'

'But you don't want to blow it either, right? I mean, better to step back than fall on your face.'

'Thanks!' She was so eager, so transparent I couldn't even be put out. Not to mention that I owed her big time. 'Either way I'll put in a word for you. "Dainen,"' I'll say, "this woman is way stronger than her scrawny self looks. She tussles like a banshee. She's got the three qualities a second unit director wants in a new cast member: she's smart, tough and desperate to make good. If you don't give her a try you'll be kicking yourself for the rest of your life." How's that?'

'Outstanding!' She grinned. 'Thanks, really. This'll make all the difference.'

'OK, but do not smother me in my sleep. Which I'm planning on doing till noon. No zazen tomorrow. Set's closed.'

We'd been half-whispering but even so I'd kept the bathroom door shut so as not to wake Leo. Now I walked, distressingly

unsteadily after my few minutes of sitting, across the hall. Aurelia
stood in my doorway questioningly until I motioned her into my
room. We sat on the futon.

I almost wished I could just thank her again and send her on
her way. But I had to ask, 'Aurelia—'

'AA.'

'A – I'm so grateful things worked out as they did, but I've
got to ask, how come you were you here, this late? Was Leo
expecting you?'

'No,' she said in a way that made me think she was considering
and deciding against giving more detail.

'I mean, it's late.'

'True.'

'You know he's still recovering, right?'

'Look, I'm sorry. I should have called first.' She started to
push herself up.

'I'm not ragging you out about manners. You're not an incon-
siderate person,' I said, as if I hadn't seen her stalk off the set
this morning. 'Why?'

'OK, OK. I wanted to talk to Leo. I've tried to see him for
days! This was the first place I came when I got to town. I was
so excited to see him. I mean, I can hardly bitch that he couldn't
be here talking to me when he was in the hospital. But, still, you
know, I really wanted to see him. I knocked. He didn't answer.
I was, well, disappointed. You know how it is when you're really
deep-down disappointed? Like there's a big hole in your gut?
By tonight I wasn't thinking. I figured maybe I could catch him
between brushing his teeth and going to bed.' She flashed an
uneasy grin. 'I – honestly – forgot he'd been injured. A little too
much seeing through my own eyes, huh?'

Seeing through my own eyes was a phrase Leo used and I
now used. It didn't mean run-of-the-mill self-centeredness. It
was believing your view of the world to be correct. Not seeing
things as they really are. More to the point, we both used it in
connection with Zen practice. 'So, are you Garson-roshi's
student?'

'Garson-roshi? Yeah, I guess.'

Student or something else? Or angling to be something more?
'From your time in Japan with him?'

'I wasn't *with him* in Japan. He was there. I was just passing through.'

I wanted – desperately – to ask her about Leo's time in Japan. Was that where he got the black mark that made him an outlier in the Zen world? That led to his being exiled to lead the nascent monastery in the woods up north where I'd met him? Was that the reason he was offered this modest nascent Zen center in a non-residential area of the city? Had he been involved in a scandal, a major breaking of a precept? A sin that no one talked about – not local Zen people, not Leo? Would he tell me if I asked? Probably. But I wouldn't ask . . . him.

Aurelia must have taken my pondering as a silent prod. 'I was in Japan to meet a guy and I had a couple of days to kill. I had to . . . I went to the temple because it was supposed to be very pretty. But, you know, it was December and Japan is just plain cold then, that kind of wet cold that seeps under your skin. Leo let me hang around in the hall after the other tourists left. He made me tea. He offered me rice and I almost ate it. Like at the very last moment I remembered the tourist talk about monks only having the rice they got from begging each day.'

I wasn't sure that would hold true for a monk tour guide in a temple. But I nodded.

'Leo was great. He spent time with me. I ignored everything he said, and you know what, he never once threw it in my face.'

'It's one of his really nice qualities. He doesn't drag the past into the present.'

'There was only one time he wouldn't help me, and that was my own fault. And now,' she caught my gaze, 'I'm good, really good – better when things work out on the set, right? I just want to tell him.'

She looked so eager, with a dash of desperate, so like a scruffy little dog, eyes wide, tail wagging, whose day I could make by just throwing the ball. One easy toss. I couldn't help wanting to do it. I glanced at the clock. 11:30 p.m. Not as late as I'd thought.

The first really good night's sleep Leo'd had in days. Whatever Aurelia's issue, it could wait. 'I don't want to wake Leo. You don't want to talk to him half asleep anyway—'

Her face went flat, like all hope had been sucked out of it. I felt terrible! And annoyed at feeling terrible. And no less terrible for that. This must be, I thought, like dealing with a sick baby when you'd do anything in the world to make her better.

How had Leo handled this? Her?

I did what I'd've guessed most everyone did. I gave in. 'Hang out here a minute and I'll slip in and check on Leo. I can grab his schedule and give you an idea when he'll be free.'

'But if he's awake—'

'It'll keep till morning, right?'

She hesitated. 'Sure.'

Once again, I pushed myself up. My knees felt like crumpled aluminum foil. There had to be a big bruise on my back and it ached anew with the effort. Plus I was getting a headache.

I knocked softly on Leo's door.

He didn't answer. I really did not want to wake him. I turned the hall light off so he'd get only the gentle illumination from my room instead of a blast from the hall bulb, and quietly turned the knob. If he didn't wake up I'd let him sleep. But it made me uneasy that he was sleeping this soundly still. He should be easing off on the night drugs by now.

I turned the handle and pushed the door quietly inward. 'Leo?' I whispered. This morning the smell of sickness had lingered in the room, but now it was almost gone, a good sign. 'Leo?'

No sound.

I stepped inside. Bent closer to his futon.

Leo wasn't there.

I flicked on his light. The blankets had been thrown back up over the mat, as if he'd just stepped out to the bathroom and would be crawling back in. As if he'd left in a hurry.

But he hadn't rushed to the bathroom in a frenzy, grabbed for the sink and knocked off the soap dish, or retched in the toilet and yanked off a wad of toilet paper. The bathroom looked fine.

And he was gone.

I did a quick survey. Leo kept his room bare. He had only a few bits of clothing. In some more formal Zen centers the roshi's assistant washes his clothes and mends the tears. Leo does that himself. But I help out enough to know what he's got. I know his habits. If he'd had a burst of healing and gone out for coffee on a night he'd be dressed in jeans, with his jacket over a sweatshirt.

His jeans and jacket were on their hooks and hanger. So, he was wearing sweats.

Aurelia was at the door, peering in, bouncing foot to foot, her short brown hair bobbing in the light.

I waved her away and shut the door.

'Hey, what's going on in there?'

'In a minute. Just give me a minute.' I held up the two pairs of sweatpants on closet hooks. New and newest.

The door pushed open. 'Darcy! What's going on?'

'Leo's gone.'

'Gone,' she repeated, and her movements stopped. 'Gone, like, to the movies? Like he'll be back soon? Like we don't have to whisper?'

'Gone, like gone. Like I don't know where he went, Aurelia!'

'I thought he was . . . When did he go?'

'I don't know. I haven't been here since morning. He could have left any time.'

'Then how do you know he's gone?'

I held up the sweatpants. 'He's wearing his pajamas.'

'Excuse me?'

'Leo owns three pairs of sweats. The newest one he keeps for times when he's around here but someone might come by and he wants to look presentable. Then there's the pair he wears the rest of the time. They're fine but they're getting thin. Maybe there's a hole or a stain on the knee. Around-the-house sweats.'

She smiled and shook her head. 'He'd never have done that in Japan. He was meticulous. Wore robes. Of course, I only saw him a couple days. Anyway, those pants are right here, in your hand, so he's not wearing them. Not here, either.'

'Exactly. He's in the third pair, the ones he sleeps in. They never leave this floor, except to go to the laundromat. We laugh about it. He would never have gotten up, left his bed unmade and walked out of here in his pajamas and' – I turned and scanned his closet floor – 'hiking boots.'

'Hiking boots?'

'Casual ones, not trekking material, but still, if you're going to stop for hiking boots, you don't put them on over your pajamas.' I slipped down onto his mat, cross-legged, as if that would somehow bring me closer to him and I'd be able to read his thoughts. 'What does this mean? Where'd he go? Why?'

'Maybe he left a note?' She was still in the doorway, still vibrating side to side, looking both eager to come full in and desperate to be gone.

'If he'd written a note it would be here.' I looked at the low table beside the bed-head. 'Zip.'

'Hidden?'

I pulled off the covers. Nothing. Lifted the futon. Not even dust.

'Who's been here? I mean, to see him?'

'No one, except Nezer, and he's been coming in the morning. I'm going to call—'

'Nezer Deutsch!'

'Yeah.'

'Why would he call him?' She was staring open-mouthed.

'He's Leo's doctor.'

'That's crazy. He's not even licensed in this state.'

'What makes you think he's not licensed?'

'Because he's not.' Seeing that didn't answer my question, she added, 'Leo told me that.'

'So you know Nezer?'

'I did for a while but, well, he found me too self-centered. You know, the kind of person who'd wake up a sick roshi at midnight because she wants to talk. The kind who'd ask a bruised woman about snagging her job.' She offered me a guilty smile that was hard to resist.

But my focus was not her; it was Nezer Deutsch. 'Leo knows him from somewhere. He insisted on him. Did he lose his license? Is there a problem? He seemed to be OK. Weird but . . . competent.'

'I'm sure he's fine. I mean, checking on a convalescent isn't brain surgery.'

'But . . . I'm going to call him.'

'At this hour, to ask about his license?'

Another time, I would have laughed. She, the toughie, seemed so appalled when it wasn't even midnight. 'To find out how dangerous it is for Leo to travel.' I opened Leo's top dresser drawer and pulled out his address book. 'Nezer first, then the police.'

TWENTY

There was still twenty minutes to go before midnight in this endless day. Aurelia offered to stay with me, in that insipid way that screams: I'm only doing this from politeness, good manners or fear of the ghost of my grandmother. I thanked her and let her go. The last thing I needed was to have her here buzzing off the walls all night. I could worry about Leo on my own.

I punched in Nezer Deutsch's number and got his voicemail. Ten minutes later he called, sounding annoyed. He'd been annoyed each time we'd spoken. 'Leo's assistant? Yes, I remember you. Did you find the person I warned you about?'

'What?'

'This morning, I specifically told you there was someone hanging around outside the, er, patient's door. I made a point of pointing that out to you! Do you not recall? There's no point in my treating a patient if those around him cannot provide a safe environment.'

'Point taken,' I said, and noted that he seemed to have missed the sarcasm. 'I'm asking about Leo now. Have you been here since the morning? Called him?'

'Of course not. I have to be back there seeing him in . . . six hours! Is there an emergency? Something the matter?'

'He's gone.'

The doctor's exhalation hit the receiver. I pictured his sallow face, his mind clicking away possibilities, counter-indications. 'If you'd paid attention to what I told you— You need a plan, a picture of how things should be. Do you have a plan? No, correct? Oh, never mind! If he's steady on his feet, he should be all right.'

'You're sure?'

'Of course not! If you'd—'

'You're not licensed here. Why did Leo call you?'

That silenced him for so long I wondered if he'd hung up and I'd missed the click. 'Why'd Leo call me? Maybe to give me the opportunity to get up before dawn day after day now that I'm not getting paid for doing it at a hospital. Maybe . . . Who the hell knows why Leo Garson does anything?'

I could have said that myself more than once.

'Listen, Assistant, if there was something I could tell you I would. Call me if he comes back and wants to see me.'

This time I heard the click loud and clear.

Then I called SFPD to report both of my assaults, though I knew the only result would be my having to wait up for a beat cop to take my statement. I wanted them to look for Leo. But there was no way they would take a missing person's report from a non-related female living with a man who has vacated a room in which there was no indication of violence. They'd be doing me a favor not to laugh.

Maybe they'd be right: that his absence was all innocent. Maybe Leo had gone for cough drops.

Maybe he'd had a relapse and lost his sense of, well, good sense, and he was wandering around nearby or on the other side of the city. Maybe . . . One thing I knew: Leo would not just leave, not in his sleeping garb, not without a note. Especially not after all that had happened this week.

Unless as his head cleared he'd realized who had attacked him and gone after him. On his own.

Of all the bad possibilities, that one frightened me the most.

And like all the others, the police would shrug it off. By the time I heard the police knock on the door I knew there was no point even mentioning these speculations.

The patrol officer, a prematurely world-weary woman with a blond ponytail, sinus issue and the name Kyul on her on uniform, knocked on the doors just as a clock somewhere on Columbus sounded midnight. She took my statement on the assaults.

'Twice?' she said. 'He followed you twice?'

'He knows where I live. He must have come around the other end of the block.'

'Why would he do that?'

We were downstairs in the hall, outside of the dokusan room where Leo had been attacked, Officer Kyul standing with pad ready, me sitting on the fourth step. The light, meant merely to prevent disaster as one moved to the better lighted kitchen, courtyard or stairs was marginally adequate. I was shivering but I couldn't tell if the cause was temperature or shock. 'Why did he come after me? Why me? Revenge, maybe? Taking out someone who'd be talking about his attack on Lila this morning?'

'Now you're saying there were three assaults?'

Four, counting mine on him outside the strip club door. But nothing would be gained by mention of that. My brother John had regaled us with 'tales of the witching hour crazies,' his own and ones from the station banter. I could almost see Kyul preparing hers. I said, 'Sendar must be an angry man. If you want my guess, he figures Lila's his possession – his love or his cash cow—'

'Or both?'

'Maybe. Probably. Anyway, I got in his way when he was chasing her and he just redirected his anger.'

'You impeded his pursuit?'

'Probably.'

'Probably?'

'She made it across Broadway before he jumped me.'

'Uh huh. You said you first spotted him coming out of an alleyway on Columbus. You were waiting for him?'

OK, so that didn't sound good. 'The man I was with said that was an emergency exit from the strip club.'

'The man you were with?'

Shit. Westcoff! 'He went to check on another exit. He wasn't around when any of this happened.'

I had the feeling a less controlled woman might have raised an eyebrow. A less tired one might have demanded his particulars. Kyul didn't. I said, 'If Sendar is still around you may find him at the Tink Pitty. You know that place.'

She laughed humorlessly.

I hesitated. *Never gratuitously offer an interrogator . . . anything.* Another John Lott-ism, one with which I concurred. Usually. 'If a woman kicked a bouncer at a sleazy club hard enough to break something—'

She looked groin-ward.

'Sadly no. Just a nose.'

'If?' she prodded with a hint of a grin.

'He probably won't be inclined to mention how it happened.

But he's going to need a doctor for that nose, not to mention the rumble here. He's probably in the ER right now.' I'd been there so often I could picture him waiting. But I definitely didn't tell her that.

'Or not. These guys aren't big on health maintenance. Chances are he's got an ice pack on his nose and you on his mind. Do you have anyone who can stay here with you tonight? Your friend, maybe, the one who went to check on the, um, other exit?'

'You're saying he'd come back to protect me now? No, actually, I'm fine. I'll lock the doors.'

'And the windows? Any entry from the roof?'

'If I panic I'll get the roshi's car. It's across Broadway a few blocks.'

Kyul just shook her head.

And I silently thanked her for her silence. 'Will you let me know if the department finds Lila? Or Sendar?'

'Sure,' she said resignedly. We both knew the odds of that happening.

I assured her again that I was fine, locked the doors after her and walked back upstairs, where I realized I was not fine at all. Suddenly every bit of horror and sadness, outrage and sense of violation, every bit of fury and gray-black despair I had kept at bay for days enveloped me. Leo's room where he'd lain, the bathroom where he'd barely been able to stand, the stairs he'd had to be helped up, the hallway downstairs where his assailant stood waiting to attack him, the dokusan room, the courtyard – it all reeked of defilement.

I couldn't stay here.

My family house was in this very city. I could be there in half an hour, eating a bowl of beef stew even at this hour. Having a shot of the whiskey favored by the old Irishmen at the old Irish bars.

I could call a cab.

I laughed. Scoring a cab anywhere but at a hotel in this city was like getting a gin and tonic in Salt Lake City.

I could call a car.

After midnight – Friday. I could learn patience.

Or – two birds here – I could do what Leo did.

TWENTY-ONE

With the familiar smell of exhaust, the vintage white BMW announced itself to the neighborhood half an hour after I'd pulled out the business card:

Hudson Poulsson
Man of all Trades

There are a number of car providers in the city but I'd have bet that Poulsson was not affiliated with any, no matter how casual. He hoisted himself out and reached for the back door but I was already headed around the front bumper. When I pulled open the passenger door I got a surprise. The car was clean. No smell of, well, anything. I'd seen it only when Renzo and I were extracting Leo from the backseat after Leo extracted himself from San Francisco General.

'Do you drive people much?' I asked after I'd given him Mom's address and let a moment pass while he realized he was going to be traversing the entire width of the city.

Unlike his last arrival, this time Hudson Poulsson had come the right way on our one-way street. As if to balance out that apparent slip into lawfulness he hung a U, drove with the lights off the half block to Montgomery, turned right into legality and switched on headlights. A couple turns later we were making a left onto Broadway. 'Otherwise,' he said in answer to my unspoken question, 'we'd never be able to get to the tunnel. Trust me, honey.'

'I've just trusted you with my life.'

'Buck off your fee. Which means I owe you.'

'No way.'

'Take it up with Garson.'

'I would if I knew where he was. He left today. No word. In his sleeping clothes.'

His head jerked – a whole head double-take – but he

swallowed whatever he was about to say and focused on the car in front.

I had the urge to search every street within walking distance. But Leo knew how to use the bus, the street car, get on BART and go to Berkeley or the airport. Even if he was right around here, it was ten to one we'd miss him. I settled for asking Poulsson to take me to the garage where Leo keeps his car.

Car in garage. No sign of use.

Poulsson swung back onto Broadway. A couple hours ago the lights had snapped and glistened; if there had been fog, they'd chased it to Dullsville. Broadway had been all sparkle and promise. But Dullsville had had its revenge. Now fog lay on the car hood like a careless moose in hunting season. Lanes were still crowded but vehicles inched along and drivers' decisions were too slow, too jerky, and much too faux-sober.

Poulsson cut in front of a shiny new car. The driver braked, honked his horn. Poulsson grinned. Then his face sagged back to normal. He looked like a bear after a bad night.

'You know Leo,' I began, 'what do you make of his just being gone?'

'That doesn't sound like Garson.'

I had the feeling he'd considered and rejected a number of more pointed comments. 'How so?'

He pulled back into the right-hand lane. More honking.

'Good thing this isn't an open carry state,' I said.

'I'm careful.' He shrugged and leaned forward onto the wheel.

I'd let him off the hook. I sat, shivering on the icy leather seat in the unheated car, alert for an opportunity to hoist him back on. From time to time cold air shot through the heater vent.

A couple more turns and we were on Geary, the fastest of the slow roads west. There was a light or stop sign every couple blocks. At the second stop, I said, 'Listen, Hudson, I'm worried about Leo. What do you think's going on?'

Four blocks later, he said, 'I've known Garson for a few years – not many. I've seen him pause before he picks up a cup – a *paper* cup – like he doesn't want to just grab it. The way he comes to the cup, you know, is important to him.'

'Like he connects with the cup.'

'That's it. I've never seen him careless.'

I thought back over the years I'd known Leo, first in his monastery up north and then here. Careless? No. 'And yet, now, without warning, he's gone.' Suddenly I was much more panicked than before I'd slid into the car, before I'd put into words how alarmingly out of character Leo's disappearance was.

Before I realized my best link to Leo's past might be Hudson Poulsson. 'So,' I insisted, 'what do you think happened to him?'

We passed through the grass- and tree-lined Park Presidio that shoots drivers north to the Golden Gate and divides the inner Richmond from the outer. I had the feeling Poulsson was counting the blocks till he could dump me, hoping he could dawdle long enough between questions to keep from telling me what he didn't want to admit.

Fat chance. Either he was going to cough up or I was going to throttle the man right here in the outer Richmond. I took a breath to control my voice and said, 'Hudson. You're worried. Why?'

He glanced right and left. Geary out here is residential. It doesn't offer the vehicular diversions of the inner boulevard.

'Why, dammit? Leo – Garson-roshi – is your friend. What do you think is going on?'

'He could be concerned about you.'

'He disappeared because he's concerned about me?'

Eyes forward, Poulsson nodded.

'And he wouldn't tell me?'

'Would you have let him go?'

'Where?'

'To danger.'

'Of course not.'

He nodded. Case closed.

Case appealed. 'Are you saying you think that's his reason? There's got to be more than that to it.'

He sighed. Drove.

'Turn here. That house over there with the light on.' Three cars were parked in front, Mom's, John's and Gary's, which meant that they were sitting at the kitchen table. We Lotts are night owls. For years John had rolled in late after long shifts and Gary pulled the adult version of all-nighters as trials approached. Gracie staggered in from dealing with threats of disease no one wanted to hear about. And Mom kept a pot of beef stew at the ready. 'Pull over here.'

Poulsson slid in front of the neighbor's driveway. 'This is what I can tell you' – *this is what I've been avoiding telling you half the way across town* – 'Garson's supposed to come with me Wednesday. He's never not come. I'll be very surprised if he doesn't show up.'

'Wednesday! He could have been dead for days by Wednesday!'

'Oh, I don't think—'

'Wednesday! He goes with *you* Wednesdays?'

'Yes.'

'Every Wednesday?'

'No, no, I wouldn't ask him to do that. Once a month.'

'You leave the city then?'

'Yes.'

'Where do you go?'

'He didn't mentioned it?' Poulsson nodded to himself. 'Not surprised. I never asked him not to, but I'm not surprised he understood. Not that I'm ashamed. Well, that's not true. I love my kids whatever. Still.'

The engine geared down. Nothing moved on the street. No house was lit but Mom's. I could picture Duffy inside the door, waiting. As I was waiting here. What *was* this man avoiding? 'Hudson?'

'Prison. I can't go more than once a month. Regulations. And it's an expense, the drive, the day off working. I'd do it more if they let me. But that once a month, it matters.'

'And Garson?'

'He rides with me. I'm glad of it. It's tense going. Good to have someone like him with me. Coming back, it's tense in a different way. Real good to have someone like that to talk to.'

'How long?'

'Sentence? Another year. Drugs. You can go up for a long, long time for a stupid mistake. I said that in the beginning. But you know, inside you realize that yourself. No need for your parent to be reminding you. Jeez, it's an eternity for someone so young.'

'How young?'

'Twenty-nine now.'

'Does Leo have visitation rights, too?'

'Clergy.'

I nodded. I felt for Poulsson. All the years my brother Mike was missing we'd wondered if he was in jail somewhere. Mom never mentioned it but she went stiff every time there was a news story about jail riots, or longer sentences, or, God forbid, a prisoner who resembled her youngest son. John used all his police connections to keep up on prisons nationwide. Gary checked whatever lawyers check. Gracie, the epidemiologist pooh-poohed jail and just agonized over previously unheard-of and incurable viruses.

I felt for Hudson Poulsson. But there was still something I wasn't getting from him. I could sit here in this cold car, keep myself from grabbing his neck and throttling him till the little ball of what he was hiding beneath the rest of this came flying out. Or I could take the easy route.

I decided to throw him to the wolves.

TWENTY-TWO

'This is Hudson Poulsson. Leo called Mr Poulsson to pick him up from San Francisco General, and he went with Mr Poulsson to see his child in prison once a month. Hudson, my family,' I said, ushering him into the kitchen while I stopped to make the oversized fuss that Duffy pretends he disdains and, of course, adores.

Poulsson was expecting a bowl of the beef stew Mom always kept ready to warm up for child or friend. I'd lured him in with that promise. He'd figured he'd eat, thank and be on the road in twenty minutes. It was, after all, nearly one in the morning. He was not expecting wolves at the table. But for the moment they were sheep's-clothing their comments and indicating a chair.

Janice, sister number two's chair, actually, though Poulsson would never know that.

The kitchen was standard mid-twentieth century. White tile, green trim. The room would have seemed large had the oval table not filled half of it. It may have been the biggest green Formica table in history. John sat at the far side from the entry door because cops always keep their eyes on the door and their backs to the wall. Gary sat opposite because a defense attorney always keeps his eyes on the cop. Gracie's chair was next to him because Gary and Gracie had been a pair growing up the way Mike and I had.

'Gracie still in Vegas?' I sotto voce'd to Gary, who responded with a micro-shrug that meant 'yes' but either he was not pleased or he didn't know any more than I did about her sudden, unexplained and uncharacteristic bolt to Nevada, and was displeased about not knowing.

The padding had been coming loose from Janice's chair as long as I could remember, but she'd insisted it was comfortable enough and should be left as it was. It was called the Berkeley chair. Poulsson probably assumed he'd been given it because it was nearest the stove, next to Mom if she ever sat down and, he might have been thinking, offered easiest access to the door in case he needed it.

Mike's chair was on the far side, appropriately in the middle where everyone was close enough to catch his eye or tap his arm and re-up what they assumed to be their special connection. But mine was right next to it because I did have the special connection. During the nearly twenty years he'd been missing the chair had stayed empty at the table. In those decades he'd often lived off the grid and had developed the annoying habit of going to bed early.

'Fall on your face?' Gary asked me conversationally as he passed me a bowl of stew. I shrugged, as I'd done all the times growing up when I'd come home bruised from misjudged leaps or wires I didn't quite have the balance to walk on. Duffy jumped up on my lap; his whiskers scratched the exact spot where I'd hit the sidewalk.

Uncharacteristically, John ignored the whole issue.

Before he could reconsider, I cut to the chase. 'Leo's gone.'

'Gone?'

'Disappeared. In the clothes he wears to bed.'

John and Gary were the wolves I'd had in mind when throwing Poulsson in. But it was Mom who sat down next to him, handed him a full bowl and said, 'You must be very worried, Hudson. It is Hudson? Not Hud?'

'Yes, ma'am,' he said, though he couldn't have been much younger than her.

'Well, you came to the right place. We'll set about finding him. John's good at that. He'll help you.'

Help *you*! Now it was *his* problem, not that he seemed to realize it.

John forced a smile, like he'd just had his fangs extracted and the anesthetic hadn't worn off. He took a swig of the tan liquid in the juice glass before him. He would, I thought, have offered Poulsson a shot of the Irish, but he was still too much cop to chance luring a driver to drink in his own family home. I poured an inch for Poulsson and one for myself. I held the glass to my mouth for a moment before I drank; the smell of the whiskey mixed with the earthy aroma of the stew and wafts of heat. If I hadn't beaten it back it would have eased open decades of memories, of the safe dangers of adolescence.

I said, 'Hudson, you told me Leo had written to you when you couldn't get out, right?' Out of where, I wanted to know, but this wasn't the time to divert to that by road.

Spoon halfway to mouth, he nodded. 'Every month, without fail. Not Zen stuff; he knows I'm Catholic. Just stuff . . .'

'Like?'

'The Giants were climbing into the lead. Candlestick was flooded for a Niners' game. Sand off the dunes blew over The Great Highway and they'd closed off the road. Just stuff.'

'You've known him for a long time then?' Gary asked. I'd seen him do this before, trying to expose the bones of a client's story amidst the loose flesh of extraneous detail.

'Oh, yeah. I helped him dig out the road to that monastery up north before we could even get lumber in.'

'Ten years ago?'

'No, less. Six, I'm thinking.'

'Christian charity?' John asked.

'For me, maybe. I'd just gotten back from Korea and I didn't know what to do and figured I owed Leo, because of the letters and all.'

'So you weren't in jail?' The words popped out of my mouth. Mom's hand shot to her mouth. She looked so appalled we all laughed, Poulsson hardest of all.

'Close enough. But no. No, these trips are my first trips and, I'll tell you, it's hard to see my little girl in that place.'

Girl!

'Leo's been leading a meditation group for women inmates?' I asked.

'Maybe, but mostly he visits, like I do.'

'Visits who?'

Poulsson's irises rose, like he was scouring the top of his eye sockets for the answer. 'Dunno. You know, I was so busy talking about Jessica I never thought to ask. And that's Leo, isn't it? Never put his own stuff first. She was in for drugs – that's all I know. But, like, in women's prison that's about half. Jessie says without drugs and boyfriends the cells would be empty.'

'Were there a lot of drugs in the monastery?' I asked.

'You'd think, huh? Up there in the back of nowhere. But no. Leo was no-nonsense about that. He told me before I got there.

Much as he needed me – and he'd still be digging if I hadn't been there – he wouldn't have let me in with a leaf or a seed. Between the sheriff assuming hippies were floating in on the fumes and the feds with their helicopters, he figured one misstep and the monastery would be history. Later, he told me he'd had a friend or two who were wanted or on the lam, laying low, you know, and he didn't even dare let them in. No one's cleaner than Leo.'

John, who had been containing himself, lost his containment. 'Poulsson, what do you know about drugs here, in the city Zen place?'

'Nothing.'

'You've seen the people who come there. They could be anyone, right? No one cards them. So who's buying and selling?'

'Like I said, I'm Catholic. I go to the cathedral. St Mary's. The new one, you know?'

Gary said softly, still holding his glass of whiskey, 'Maybe no drugs, but the traffic from Broadway, the girls, the pimps, maybe Leo ran afoul of them. D'you think? Did he say anything? Long rides in the car like you two had, it's a time when guys talk about things. Who could Leo trust as much as you? You, his friend. When you're in a position of authority like his, you really need someone whose only connection is to you. An old friend.'

Poulsson sipped the whiskey. The man looked anxious to help Gary. 'I don't know. This is outta leftfield and maybe, probably, it's not connected at all, but one day two months – no, no, it was three months – I remember because we were talking about the Giants and the season had just started.'

John's teeth were jammed together so hard spit was leaking out one side. But Gary smiled and nodded for Hudson to go on.

'I asked him about karma. You know, we all think we know what it means, because, well, we all use the word like we know. You know?'

Gary nodded with real-looking enthusiasm.

'But Leo said karma is cause and effect. You do something, something happens. Maybe not what you intended. But once you've done it, things happen, you know, and they go on out of your control.'

John refilled his glass. He looked like he was using all his restraint not to down it in one gulp.

'Like, Leo said, you're on the top of a mountain. It's winter. You throw a snowball at a friend. It missed and starts rolling down the hill.'

'Snowballing,' John muttered.

'Exactly!'

'And the connection?' Gary prompted.

Poulsson hesitated. The man looked lost. 'Oh, jeez, I don't know. I thought I knew. I . . . oh . . . Jeez. I'm sorry.'

John was purple. He took a deep breath, opened his mouth—

Mom shot him a look. She put a hand on Hudson's shoulder and after a moment said, 'Well, we all know about thoughts slipping away, don't we? But Hudson, there was a connection, something Leo said to you in the car that afternoon in the spring when the Giants' season had just started and you two—'

'Oh, yeah. Now I remember. He said sometimes you think you are doing the right thing and the consequences go haywire. I said I hoped he wasn't talking about me. He wasn't.'

'And?' Gary asked after a couple moments.

'That's it.'

That was too much for John. 'Poulsson, where the fuck is he?'

'Leo?'

'Yeah, Leo!'

'I wish I knew. Truly. I wish. I don't.'

'You go anywhere else together? He talk about friends? Problems? Someone out to get him?'

Poulsson kept shaking his head. 'No one would hurt Leo, I mean, not intentionally.'

'But someone did. A man clubbed him. Who, Poulsson?'

Hudson shrank back behind his bowl, the symbol of the hospitality that had been offered and dragged away. The man was quivering. His lips were trembling.

Before Mom could speak, John turned on me. 'You! Look at you. You look like the loser in a cat fight.'

'I know. It'd be worse if a woman in the courtyard hadn't saved me. I didn't even see her—'

'That's it! The connection!' Poulsson beamed at Mom. 'Leo said occasionally there'd been a homeless guy sleeping in the courtyard. Not the same guy, but, you know, different guys, occasionally.'

John bit his lip.

'Leo felt bad about the homeless guys but he couldn't let them come in and sleep in the zendo because, well, you know.'

Gary and Mom nodded. John sat stony-faced.

'So Leo chose the middle way, sort of. He didn't hassle them.'

'Yeah, fine,' John said and scraped his chair back in just the way Mom had told him not to year after year.

But she didn't bite. 'Go on, Hudson.'

'Leo said he suspected that the guy there then – in the court-yard at night – wasn't really homeless. That he was there for some other reason. I said to him, "You mean, like a lookout?" and he said maybe. He didn't know.'

'I asked him what he was going to do about it. He said he just had suspicions, nothing firm. He was going to be alert.'

'He never mentioned anything to me!' I said.

'He didn't want to put you in the position of having to make a choice about the situation.' Poulsson looked apologetic, as if he was channeling Leo. And he looked confused.

What Leo had meant, of course, was that he didn't want me to have to chance mentioning it in front of John and take the consequences, or be constantly alert not to. 'Thanks.'

John turned to me. I tensed for his reaction. But what he said had nothing to do with Leo and courtyard security. 'What about that reporter you were with?'

'Westcoff?' Of course John would have heard about it. I filled in the rest. 'Westcoff's doing a story on human trafficking and drug smuggling. We were hoping to spot the guy who attacked me and Westcoff saw one of this guy's victims escaping.'

'Jeez, Darce. Guy attacks you on your grounds. Leo's grounds. He's involved in trafficking. Leo's giving his victim a safe haven. He comes after you. You and Wonder Zen Woman rout him. Don't you think he might be pissed at Leo?'

'The police are looking for him.'

'They need to be breathing down Westcoff's neck to find him.'

I had thought the wolves would devour Hudson Poulsson, but he was settling in like a second family dog. A sweet man who grieved for the suffering of his daughter and drove people all over. The man was almost too good to be true. So good, in fact, the wolves not only didn't devour him, they offered him the guest bed.

In part that was because their focus had changed. It was Westcoff their teeth were itching for.

TWENTY-THREE

I woke up, finger-in-the-electric-socket panicked. Out by the ocean the fog's a near-constant neighbor. I blinked and blinked again, and still I could barely make out the smudges where I'd peeled off the remains of the planets and stars I'd slept under my freshman year in high school, before Saturn fell on my nose one Thanksgiving morning. That day I'd slept through the collapse, so I have only Mike's word that he didn't stage the photo that led to me being called Saturn-snout all day.

Sleeping in the room where you grew up coats you with childhood, no matter how adult you think you've become. This morning the door had inched open and Duffy hustled in and leapt, grunting, onto the bed. (Mom's bought him a two-step foam ladder to climb on her bed!)

'You are the most spoiled dog in all of San Francisco,' I said, scratching his head.

Slowly, the night before shimmied into focus. The panic about Leo solidified. I reached for my phone, checked messages. Just one, from Dainen Beretski. He'd be in the production room all day. Unsaid was: so should I. I agreed. There's no holiday when deadline threatens.

But fat chance.

Not unless I connected with Leo pronto. I hit Leo's number, got his voicemail message.

'Damn!' I snapped up to sitting.

Duffy grunted.

Leo was not answering his phone. Could be a dozen reasons. The same dozen that hadn't held water last night. Now I remembered my wanting to go back to the zendo then, to be there in case—

'In case what?' John had said. 'If he walks in fine, he's not going to want to see you. If he doesn't walk in there's no use you being there.'

'But if he's injured or—'

'I'll have the guys keep an eye on the place.'

'A drive by every hour? I don't think—'

'Trust me.'

'Yeah, Darce,' Gary'd said, 'hovering, that's one thing you can count on him for. You'll be lucky if he isn't up a ladder and peeking in Leo's window every hour.'

'What about—'

'Westcoff? I've got the guys on that. If they can't find him, you can't. Go to bed.'

And if Leo was on the trail of his assailant? If he was trying to find him without being spotted? I hadn't even bothered to ask.

I'd wanted . . . But when I'd shoved myself up from the table, a wave of exhaustion hit so strong that I felt wobbly. Even I had had to admit that a night's sleep was the only option.

Now, this morning, I left Duffy burrowing into the warm spot I'd abandoned, pulled on my jeans, checked the closet – Mom keeps a rotating array of clothes for emergencies or poor planning of her offspring – and extricated a silver-blue T-shirt that was Gracie's. Bathroom, breakfast and then Poulsson and I were on our way. Mom was gone, which I'd already assumed when Duffy didn't bother to leave the bed.

Fog covered Hudson Poulsson's old BMW-like gray pudding. Sections of the windshield opaque'd as soon as the wiper moved off. Poulsson bent toward it, fingers white on the steering wheel. The car was January cold but he didn't try the heater and I didn't ask why. It could have been six in the morning or ten. 'I'll go through his room,' I said, speaking of Leo, 'but if I don't find anything you're going to have to call your daughter.'

'It's not that easy.'

'Then you should start the process as soon as we get to the zendo.'

'She doesn't like to talk about other prisoners. It's dangerous. She—'

'Hudson!'

He nodded and kept driving east, less intent on driving than avoiding my demands.

But he promised to answer if I called – I believed him – and I got out in front of the zendo and watched him drive away.

The street was empty. Peaceful or ominous. Renzo's Caffe was closed. I stood looking down toward its empty gray windows and then turned and strode into the courtyard, stopping to scan the low stone wall, the inner side where the homeless slept, where Renzo had lain.

For an instant the key stuck, then the madrone door swung free and I stepped into the entryway. 'Leo?'

The syllables seemed to ring in a bell of emptiness. I glanced in the dokusan room, the kitchen, the zendo, before running upstairs and checking Leo's room, hoping he might be asleep. He wasn't. Not there.

Other rooms were empty.

I turned back to Leo's room, stood in the doorway. Where to begin to search?

Without thinking, I turned and walked down to the zendo, lit the candle, bowed to my cushion and sat. Not facing the wall – facing into the room that had been the center of my life here.

Thoughts raced at me. I could feel my shoulders quivering, my chest cold with foreboding. With effort, I let those thoughts go and focused on the flow of my breath, wondered how long Leo had been gone, forced my attention back to my breath, wondered why he would leave, came back to my breath, wondered why someone would force him to leave. Back to breath. What he could have abandoned or placed strategically that would give me some hint? And breath. And breath.

There's a moment when you sit that your body shifts down a notch, that the flow of breath and the awareness of sound grows stronger, that you are not yanked around by each fear-laden thought. A certain calm, focus. When that time came I sat for a few more minutes then got up, bowed to my cushion, walked out of the zendo up to the phone.

Poulsson answered on the first ring.

'It's Aurelia, isn't it?' Aurelia, who'd lifted weights every day, who'd run when she could, did chin ups in her room. Who had made it her business to come out in good shape. Who'd gone to Japan to meet a guy. Who Leo would not shelter in the monastery up north.

I could hear him swallowing over the phone. 'Hudson, she told me about working out, even in her room. Yes or no?'

TWENTY-FOUR

Finding a person you hardly know and now realize you know less well than you assumed you did is no cakewalk, particularly in San Francisco, where there are pockets of homogeneity in pretty much any neighborhood. Even the Barbary Coast, a tiny boutique commercial district, had been de-gentrified by us, and we by the homeless guy in the courtyard. Aurelia Abernathy had been released from prison very recently. So recently that she had not yet been able to see the person she most wanted to be with. She'd been here at the zendo every day this week trying to get to Leo. If anyone had her address, it would be him.

I stepped into Leo's room. Garson-roshi's room. Of course, I needed to finger through every drawer like a hotel thief on the make for jewels. Leo was missing! This room was my only lead to Aurelia and, I hoped, to Leo himself. I had to examine every notebook, pad, scrap of paper, take apart his bedding, root through his dirty laundry. Long as he'd been missing, there was no chance he'd just walked off.

And yet I stood, unable to invade the privacy of my teacher. Part of the unspoken covenant of our relationship was that I focused on his needs and he focused on my Zen practice. I brought him tea; he listened to me as I circled around my fears, grumbled about work or the lack of it. He found my koans therein.

That was exactly what had happened in the dokusan room a minute before he was attacked. What had he said to me?

If you meet the Buddha in the road, kill the Buddha.

If I had mentioned that interchange to the police, they'd have veered so far into leftfield they'd have been paddling in the bay.

The dokusan room door had been shut while Garson-roshi and I talked; there was no chance of the assailant overhearing us.

But more to the point, *Kill the Buddha* did not mean to actually *kill* the Buddha. It was a koan well-known among Zen students. Rely on nothing. Give up the thing you so thoroughly believe will make you happy. Don't hang onto anything. Give up even your desire to give up.

Garson-roshi had offered me that koan when I was grumbling about work.

Give up work?

Give up the illusion of a steady, reliable employment doing what I most wanted?

Give up picturing Hollywood as I wanted it to be?

No, not as easy as that.

Give up the righteous pleasure of annoyance?

There are times you know you've hit the truth just by the awful feeling you get.

Give up the righteous pleasure of annoyance not just in work, but in the rest of my life. My brother John stepped front and center.

Rats!

Give up being furious that he'd made a habit of circling the block in the middle of the night on his way home from work? Give up 'What if I'd been coming home with a guy? Would I be bare light bulb'd about him at dinner?'

Give up my indignation at the alarm guy John had sent who'd charged into the zendo in the middle of zazen and announced he'd come to protect us from coming home to find emptiness?

Give up the constant, visceral irritation of suspecting I was constantly being watched?

And if you give up doing that, what are you? I could almost hear Garson-roshi asking. *What are you then?*

Nothing.

For an instant, with the whole brouhaha scooped away, I felt just nothing. I stood there, outside Garson-roshi's door in the empty hallway, feeling empty.

'I guess John's got reasons—'

Not important. Don't go to leftfield. The cops are already there. I could picture Leo laughing.

What he meant was don't fill the empty space with a different set of assumptions.

'I don't see how—'

Be alert!

By which he meant spot those thoughts coming in.

I stood for another moment, still outside Garson-roshi's door. It would take a while to give up the feeling of being watched.

I swallowed, reached for the knob and walked into his room. The place was just as it had been before – covers jumbled off the futon, a little buckwheat pillow at an angle, books piled by the head of the bed, closet door shut, dresser drawers shut. Car keys in a green bowl on the dresser.

I went to his address book first. He'd handed that to me before. No scraps of paper with addresses, no odd phone numbers with no names. Nothing even crossed out.

There she was: AA. The prefix of the phone number served the East Bay – where the federal prison was.

A month ago this might have been a find. Now it was nothing. She'd been there. She wasn't now. I had no more idea of her San Francisco address than before. And if Leo had known it, he would have written it in this book.

Which meant she hadn't told him. Yet. So, she probably hadn't been released long.

There had to be halfway houses in the city. Some more likely than others. John might know. I could call him and test out my intent to give up being annoyed.

Or, knowing John, I could just walk outside.

I glanced in Leo's closet again, and at the surfaces in the room, but did not open a single drawer. I hoped I was making the right decision. If I was wrong . . .

Then I trotted downstairs and into the courtyard.

'No need to pretend to be asleep,' I said, tapping the 'homeless' guy on the arm. 'You and I are going to make a deal.'

TWENTY-FIVE

The 'homeless' guy shrugged and rolled over like a bear in winter.

I grabbed his jacket and shook him. 'How the hell did Leo walk out of here and you not notice?'

'Huh?'

'Skip the act. I could be on the phone to John right now. He's wasting his money on a loser who cannot even lie in the courtyard and keep his eyes open.'

'I dunno wha—'

'Forget it!' I whipped my phone out of my pocket.

Of course, he was protesting before I got my finger to the screen. He was saying, 'Deal?'

'Right. The deal is you answer my questions, do what I tell you and I let you walk away. I do not tell my brother what a useless piece of litter you are.'

'Hey, I—'

'Take it or don't. I'm on a tight schedule.'

Of course, he took it. Pushing himself up was like a volcano readying itself to erupt. Rumbling and sending specks of debris flying. He discarded the sleeping bag he'd had bunched under his chest and the blanket. And a long, heavy wool coat meant for the good life in the Northeast. And a scarf. He stood in jeans and a maroon sweater. The process transformed the old winter bear to a skinny guy with matted brown hair, the better to sleep on the pavement on. A month of decent meals, off substance, an hour in the shower and he might be good to go. More accurately, knowing John's minions, he once was good to go. Now the smell of sweat-dried wool and dust cocooned us.

I shot a glance at the cold, rough, filthy pavement. 'How long have you been on this job?'

'Let's see. Almost a month.'

'Every night?'

'Nah. I got a Wednesday sub.'

'Other than Wednesdays you're here full time?'

'Oh yeah. Eleven to seven.'

'But you've been here later.'

He shrugged. 'I overslept.'

I couldn't help it. I laughed. 'How is it that John knows you?'

'Professionally.'

'He arrested you for . . .?'

'Petty.'

Petty covered an array of small crimes – shoplifting, marijuana, boosting off the back of a truck. The day laborer tasks of the small crime world, generally done by men, and women, who'd as soon labor on the right side of the law if work presented itself. My brother had been on the force for thirty-some years. He had a stable of informants and off-the-book guys. Keeping an eye on me this last year, I realized, had provided a few of them employment. Outraged as I had been at my brother's presumption and the intrusion, these minions of John's had occasionally been a convenience for me.

'What's he paying you, Mr . . .?'

'Vessie. Martin Vessie. Twenty an hour.'

To lie awake on the pavement eight hours a night! 'That's all?'

Vessie shrugged. 'He ran interference with a proprietor I, uh, ran afoul of.'

Good for John. Criminal rehab . . . 'So, Mr Vessie, how is it you overlooked Leo Garson leaving here yesterday?'

'Not my shift.' The words flew out of his mouth almost before I'd finished asking. And he was proud!

'So, you're saying Leo Garson left here between seven in the morning and eleven at night?'

'I guess. You don't expect strong-armed kidnapping in the middle of the day.'

And yet . . . 'What about when Sendar attacked me right here in the courtyard? Not your shift?' Soupçon of sarcasm there.

'He must've been a light foot, right? D'you hear him running up behind you? By the time I woke – looked up – Aurelia was kicking ass for you.'

'So you did nothing?'

'Hey, who do you think called the cops?'

While I'd been faking the 911 call, Vessie was off somewhere making a real one. Still . . . 'He trotted off. You couldn't have grabbed him?'

'Hey, I'm paid to watch. I got a herniated disc.'

Hard to get good help! I leaned back against the low wall. If Vessie was being straight, then Leo had gone missing after morning zazen. The later in the morning, the more street traffic there would have been. Offices and boutiques would have been open. Though with Renzo gone the main eye on our place would have been missing. Still, it was not a time you'd drag a man across the sidewalk and stuff him into a getaway vehicle.

Gun to his side? That was possible. Metal gun. Emotional gun. Two people walk to a car in the middle of the day. Hardly a noteworthy event.

But Vessie had slipped in one noteworthy item. Aurelia. 'So you know Aurelia. From prison?'

'No.'

'But you recognized prison in her, right?'

'Nah. She spotted me. Last week,' he added, as if used to providing dates of occurrences.

'What was she doing here last week?'

'Knocking. Must've been none of you home.'

'Between eleven and seven in the morning?'

'Nah. Later. After breakfast. I forgot my bag.' He shot a look of disdain at the filthy sleeping bag. 'Took me a couple days to get this one authentic. I didn't want to spend bucks on a new one to destroy. So I came back. Nine-sixteen . . . a.m. I checked my watch because I was figuring I'd been gone too long and it'd've been snatched. Nine-sixteen. No one home. She turns around, spots me and recognizes me.'

'From?'

'Here.' He could have added, *Idiot!*

'She'd seen you here before, during the night?'

'Guess so.' Again, he could have added . . .

'Did you see her?'

'Well, yeah. That's what I'm paid for.'

Yeah, right.

'She went to the door like she was going to knock and then she stopped, like all of a sudden she realized it was the middle of the night. Or maybe she saw the light on in your window.'

He knew which window was mine? That creeped me out more than anything he'd said. 'Then what did she do?'

'Left. It was the middle of the night.'

'Where'd she go?'

It was a throwaway question but he hesitated too long before his throwaway *don't know.*

'But you do know where she is, right? You didn't find out then. You found out later.'

He shifted from foot to foot in worn hiking boots that looked two sizes too big. 'Not really.'

'Hey, we've got a deal here. No chiseling. Where does she live?'

'I don't know which house.'

'What do you know?'

'OK. She was at that halfway house out in the Richmond, you know?'

I nodded, though I didn't. 'And?'

'She didn't want to stay there. Said it was full of ex-cons. Like that shoulda been a surprise. But, she said, she was done with that life. Said she was never going back inside. Even the people she liked she didn't want to see again, ever. That life was over. She'd kept herself in shape – sure looked like it from the way she lit into that guy coming after you. You know, like a year in lock-up let loose there – and she was hot to be in the movies. Do stunts, like you do. She wanted to "take chances, bust ass, fly." That's a quote from her. She intended to get a spot in a house where people like her – movie people – stayed. Next time I saw her, she shot me a wink. I figured she'd done it.'

'Which place?'

'I told you all I know.'

'OK.'

'So we're even. You're not going to rat me out? I can keep my gig?'

'Right. But you do understand that you're reporting to me now. Got it?'

His expression said, in sequence: *What! Oh, shit! John'll have my ass. Lott's sister here, she's as crazy as Lott. Crap! I'm between a rock and a hard place. Pavement collapsing under my feet. What choice . . .? Tell her what she wants to hear. That's it!*

'Got it.'

TWENTY-SIX

'How is he?' I'd gotten hold of Renzo's niece.

Her uncle, she'd reported, had been released from the hospital – bones healing – and was staying with her. 'Can't keep him out of the kitchen. He oughta be sitting in a chair watching TV. He won't. Either he's going to do himself an injury or we're going to burst from all the pastry.'

'Tell him I asked after him.'

'He's been wanting to talk to you, but with all the calls for him – relatives, friends, doncha know, the phone never cools. If he wasn't off at the doctor you'd be leaving a message.'

'Why did he want to talk to me?'

'To find out what's going on. It's driving him crazy that there was a fight, one that he was in, and he doesn't know what happened. I mean, he wants the skinny on every single thing that went down. You know Uncle Renzo.'

I laughed. 'I'll tell him every detail when he reopens the cafe. We'll send in the participants and the observers and even the cops, one by one, and he can milk them dry. Tell him.'

'Believe it. Whoops, gotta go! Kids!'

I clicked off. Then I called my agent to find out if he knew where in the Mission district stunt doubles stayed. But he had no intention of talking housing.

'Where are you? Beretski's been on the horn to me three times since midnight. One of them at four a.m. The last, an hour ago. Guy's flipping his rug about you.'

'What does he want?'

'You! There! In the production room. Sweating.'

'What'd you tell him?'

'Are you crazy? At four in the morning? It went to voicemail. He's hair-on-fire, but listen, Darcy, you make this gag work and you're golden. Blow it and he'll spew mud over you so deep archeologists won't find you for a thousand years.'

'OK. OK. I'm on my way. Literally. I'm walking. Hear the

traffic? But tell me, what do you know about a hotel, rooming house, rooms for rent, whatever place an aspiring stunt double might live, in the Mission?'

'I'll get back to you. Really. Gotta go. Really. It's Beretski – on the other line. I gotta fall all over myself with him for you.'

The phone clicked off in the middle of Montgomery Street. I walked the half block to Broadway. The street looked like sin gone stale. The clubs were closed, marquee lights off, flashing boobs and neon nipples gone dark. Fog grayed it all and held in the night chill.

Moving east, downhill, I picked up my pace, counting on the rhythm of my feet to provide a medium for decision. The only lead, tenuous as it was, to Leo, was Aurelia. I needed to—

My phone buzzed. My very fine agent!

'Two. Twenty-third and Valencia. Nineteenth and Guerrero. You want the numbers?'

'Yes.'

He read them out, repeated them, and I wrote on my inner arm. 'I got Beretski calmed,' he added. 'If you show up in the next ten minutes, he still will be.'

'I will. Thanks. You're the best.'

'I know.' And he was gone.

There was just time to get hold of Aurelia – not throw out questions on the phone where I couldn't judge her reactions, but lure her over here for coffee, maybe within the hour. I was counting on her to have a direct and solid lead; I shouldn't, but I was. Because there wasn't anything else.

I called the place on Twenty-third. A man answered. He'd never heard of Aurelia Abernathy. At the second place, on Nineteenth, a woman picked up. She didn't recognize the name, hadn't seen anyone of her description, hadn't taken on a new tenant in a month.

'Are you sure?' I said in desperation.

The woman just clicked off.

A boa of fog wrapped around my neck. It seemed appropriate. If I hadn't promised to be at work in – now – five minutes, I'd have trudged. Trudged through the mire of all ends being dead.

Instead, I ran, faster and faster downhill, swung around the

last corner and, panting, pushed open the door into the production room.

Right in the middle of the production room was Aurelia
Abernathy. In an army-green sleeveless T-shirt, black-and-white
print tights and red shoes. In case Dainen Beretski missed her.
Not likely, though; she was at his shoulder. Staring wide-eyed
up at him, taking in his every word. From the looks of him those
words were 'I'm busy!'

To him she was one more crazy-making detail in a day
crammed with them.

To me she was a fluttering veil to screen off my late arrival.
'Hey, Dainen,' I said. 'Want me to tell Aurelia about the changes
in the gag?'

He was looking at his phone, at a picture of the sun on a
weather app. 'Sun! Dammit! We're going to have to— Darcy,
yeah, sure, take her.'

Yesterday I would have marveled at Aurelia letting that brush-
off roll off her back. Now she offered me the same eager smile
she'd beamed at Beretski as we squeezed past a disassembled
block of lights and a pair of harried-looking guys holding pipe
and tapping. Buzzes of intense talk mixed with excitement and
panic, and a woman rasped out a demand for more light; deep-
throated groans and hurricane-worthy sighs followed.

'Hey, Margo.' I nodded to the continuity woman. Without
looking up from her notes, she moved her head. 'Fog.' She
kneaded the word as if expecting to pull it into a more promising
shape.

'Huh?' Aurelia muttered.

'It's going to be sunny the next couple days,' I said, keeping
her moving toward the far corner. 'The scenes they've shot have
been in fog. Now, even if we can get permission to be at the
location before five a.m., Dainen and Margo don't know if there'll
be enough cloud cover. If not, they have to decide if the shots
can be saved in post-production. Or are they trash? More to the
point, how can we shoot the gag here in sunlight and still have
it work?' I pointed to a photo shot up Lombard yesterday, angled
to capture the street and the sky. Gray sky had turned it black
and white. Fog-veiled windows were opaque. Aurelia bent
forward, squinting.

I said, 'How often did Leo visit you in prison?'

I was expecting shock. But I'd underestimated her, or what she'd learned in the lock-up. She didn't move. She let a breath pass and said, without inflection, 'Every month.'

'Wednesdays?'

'Yes.'

'How long?'

'The whole time. Eighteen months.' She held her shoulders tight – they were more developed than I'd realized – but her cap of curls quivered from the effort.

'Why?'

She snapped up to face me. 'What's your point, Darcy?'

I glanced around the room to remind her of my position here. 'Answer the question.'

'Ask him.'

'You tell me.'

The moment froze – she, I, the air between us – then, as if that instant disappeared and a new one replaced it, as if firewood had been replaced by ash without any interim of burning, she said, 'Kindness. He did it from kindness.' There was a touch of regret in her voice.

'Not meditation?'

'Nah. I tried that. I'm not the sitting still kind.' She sighed and leaned back, her butt on the table edge. 'If you're asking if we were lovers? Ever? No. Do I love him? Of course. Does he love me? Love's not the right word.'

I nodded. For good or bad Leo cared about anyone who gave him the chance. Even those who didn't.

At the end of the Saturday lectures we chant the Four Vows. The First Vow is 'Beings are numberless; I vow to save them.' Many people take that as a play on words, but for Leo it's life. His focus is the dharma in, as far as I can tell, all things. All beings. 'And yet, he's not visiting anyone else in prison.'

'He felt bad.'

Leo had been kept at the periphery of the Zen establishment. Before I knew him there'd been some scandal, misdeed, a breaking of vows serious enough to taint him for years. Yamana-roshi, my old teacher in New York, had mentioned the existence of the taint but not the substance. Leo had never given voice to it at all. And, curious as I was, I never asked. But now I prodded, 'Because?'

'Look, I don't see—'

What I really needed to find out was where Leo was. Was I taking the chance of pushing her hard enough to send her running to satisfy my curiosity? I could have moved between her and the door. Instead, I said, 'Try standing like this, shifting your balance from foot to foot. No, don't balance on both feet – shift the weight so it's on one foot and the other is touching the floor but loose.'

She moved slowly back and forth as if getting the movement – definitely taking my point about balance. The balance needed in this gag. My role in hiring for this gag.

'Like I said the other day' – she was shifting easily now – 'I met Leo in Japan. He was in a monastery. I had a few days to kill. He assumed I was interested in the dharma. I let him think that. I was young. Long straight hair, blond back then, the whole "look." I was used to guys coming on to me. Leo never made a move and that was a kind of relief.'

'Because?'

'I was waiting for a contact – drugs. The common story. I was wowed by the fast life, the easy money. I thought a little packet would be an easy carry back home. I had the look; I assumed I could handle customs men. I'd already gotten a pass in a couple countries when I hadn't been carrying anything. I was . . . a fool.'

My hand started toward her shoulder to support, to comfort. I stopped. 'That doesn't explain about Leo.'

'He'd told me those were his last days in Japan. He was heading home to take over a monastery in California. I asked if I could write. He gave me the address.'

'Did you write?'

'No. I got arrested. I jumped bail and ran. I figured Leo's monastery in the woods would be the perfect place to hide. I hitched a ride up there. Walked down the road to the place. The road's endless.'

I nodded. I'd driven down that road. 'Walking! Must have taken hours.'

'Yeah, I was next to dead when I dragged in. I told Leo I was desperate. I'd do whatever he wanted. I just needed to lay low for a while.'

I'd seen Leo take big chances on people, put common wisdom aside because he believed they could be helped. I'd watched him listen and listen to tales that would have numbed me unconscious because he believed they covered a thread of wanting to 'see.'

'So he let you stay?'

'No, he did not! I begged, I cried, the whole array. He felt bad for me; I know that. But he said he could not have police issues there, that that would destroy the monastery.'

'He turned you in?' I asked, stunned.

'No. He took me to the bus stop.'

'And?'

'I called an old boyfriend and stayed with him. The "look" and all, you know. He, the boyfriend, assumed, well, you know, he assumed what he wanted to believe . . . that giving him my body meant giving myself, you know? And then the cops found me and arrested me. I ended up in prison. He didn't, but it ruined his career. And you can believe he didn't write to me in prison!'

I leaned back against the wall. The rumble and buzz around the room suddenly seemed very loud. Margo was jabbing a finger at something on her table. A black-garbed, make-up-free assistant nodded like a bobble doll.

'AA, when did you get out?

'Eight days, three hours and' – she glanced at her watch – 'thirteen minutes ago. I didn't expect Leo to put me up. He'd already told me there was nowhere for guests. I said I had a lead to a halfway place. When I got there it was disgusting.'

'Couldn't you stay with a friend?'

'I didn't know anyone but the guy who didn't visit. He'd have been glad to have me, but he'd've figured I owed him night and day, you know? I might as well have stayed in my cell.

'I was desperate to see Leo, this time, actually for some guidance. I said that, but who knows whether he believed me – the boyfriend, I mean. I was so dying to see Leo I showed up in the middle of the night and only a last-minute strike of decency kept me from pounding on the door. I just wanted to be able to hug him without guards leering. Without "Time's up, Abernathy." So now you know it all. Satisfied?'

Stunned. Sorry. And yet, I realized, not a whit closer to finding Leo. I told her that.

'Still? He's still gone? The cops haven't found him?'

'No. Grown man; room with no sign of struggle. Not going to be top priority. So, I'm asking you if you have any idea where he might be.'

She stood, looking as stunned as I had been. 'Where he is? No. I barely know where I am in this city. Let me think about it. Maybe he said something. Yeah, let me go find some coffee and scour my brain.'

I could have reminded her there was coffee right here.

Instead I waited a couple minutes and followed her.

TWENTY-SEVEN

Aurelia took the long strides of the free. She'd definitely kept herself in shape in prison and now she was moving fast.

But she was no match for me, not with my weekly dance workout, the super stretch session, gymnastics, lift-and-sculpt, rope-and-wall climb and the occasional classes I take just in case I'm neglecting some movement or muscle group in some area of my body I've forgotten. Scarce as stunt gigs are I don't plan to miss out because I can't do a pinky lift or a back flip. Or, as required in a commercial that didn't pan out, beat out a NFL running back. So I wasn't even winded following Aurelia.

Where was she going? Not for coffee, that was certain. The production room was near the Embarcadero with its renovated piers, parks, cafes and take-out joints. I'd assumed she'd head there.

Instead, she hurried uphill back into the city.

Keeping up? No problem. Tailing without being spotted? A whole 'nother issue. She headed west on Broadway. Buildings rose from the edge of the sidewalk with few recessed doorways to whip into, and the street was morning-after empty. The wind off the Pacific snapped leaves and sent bits of paper flying. My hair swirled in my eyes. I fingered inside my pockets for a rubber band but when I surveyed the plunder in my hand I found only a penny, a dime and a tissue.

And Aurelia was gone! Vanished.

Did she really know where Leo was? Did that mean she'd kidnapped, or lured him out of the zendo? Based on this great bond of theirs after a couple of days' meeting in Japan years ago? Or did that bond exist only in her mind? But there were prison visits. They could have been based on love, or as she said, kindness. What did I really know about her?

I stared at the spot where she'd been. Next to an alley. One of the many alleys in this area.

I knew this one. A dead end. I moved closer. Then I saw the

doorway right beyond it, and through the store windows Aurelia. She was facing the door, back to the street, looking at her phone. Punching in a number. I edged closer. If she turned she'd be in my face.

But her attention was on the phone. 'No!' she snapped. 'It's got to be today, it's got to be now!'

I held my breath and leaned closer.

'Wherever you want. Look, I'm doing this as a favor to you. A big fucking favor.'

I could hear the grumble of a voice answering but there was no chance of making out words.

'Look, I'm meeting you, coming to you; that's what you've been after. You get to ask me your questions. You win!'

A meeting to answer questions?

'Not that late,' she was saying. 'I've got prep to deal with. I'm doing a big stunt tomorrow.'

Really?

'No! Never mind! Go wherever you want. But I'm going to be there in ten minutes.'

She clicked off so fast I had to jump for the alley. She shot across the street, skirting a motorcyclist. The driver flipped her the bird. If she noticed, she didn't react but double-timed it on up the street. I trailed her on my side, watching for a chance to cross and not have squealing brakes proclaim my presence. She dashed across feeder streets, oblivious to shortcut drivers. The light turned against her at Columbus but she didn't break stride. Horns blasted; fingers flew; one guy opened his window and yelled. I gave up worrying about her spotting me and focused on keeping her in sight while managing to survive.

Finally, she turned left.

I wasn't about to lose her now! I ran into the four-lane roadway, arms waving to stop two cars eastbound and a westbound cab. And when I swung around the corner she'd taken she was, once again, nowhere in sight.

And I was in an alley, in one of those areas in the city where neighborhoods lose their distinction, back into each other without order or control. Where a turn of the corner is a turn of fortune, a shift from safe to suspicious. Here heavy, window-less storage buildings that had been consistently shoved to the outer edges of Chinatown, stained with a century of dirt and exhaust stood next to narrow and closed shops with Chinese lettering, a one-story wooden warehouse: *LamaPaca*, another, windowless, signless, emitting the aroma of coffee and citrus. Dumpsters sidled by garbage cans. Weeds died in the cracks of the pavement. There were dozens of places to hide.

But Aurelia hadn't planned on fading out of sight when she dressed this morning in her black-and-white print tights and red running shoes. I spotted her halfway down the alley, taking a few steps, eyeing the blank backs of buildings, inhaling as if to draw in this new data and moving on. She couldn't be looking for numbers. There weren't any. The roadway slanted into a crack at the center. Big chunks of pavement had long ago been jostled nearly free, sharp edges thrust up at odd angles. It was a road only safe for a four-wheel drive or those who knew when to swerve.

Aurelia stopped behind a three-story stucco structure. The top two stories hung out over what might have been a carport. No vehicles were there. The building was set back relative to its neighbors so that the windowless walls on either side created a courtyard of sorts, the kind that might be an exercise yard in prison. It had no decoration on any of the three walls, save the windows and a flat-against-the-wall ladder that must have passed as a fire escape on the building in the middle.

'This it?' I said, coming up behind her.

She started, but looked relieved. 'Yeah.'

'Where is he? Leo?'

'All I got was a building with an escape ladder and faded red and white paint.'

'Can't be two.' Painters had tried to cover the red facade with white, starting from bottom to top, and given up midway. 'Which floor is Leo on?' I glanced side to side at the block of a building. 'How do we get in? From the front?'

'No, that's a different building.'

'What's this place? Storage unit?'

'Could be.'

I nodded. With the real estate prices in the city, living in a storage unit had shifted from 'a step above the gutter' to 'reasonable short-term option.'

A single metal sheet of a door led from the empty car park

into the building. The only windows were on the top two floors. 'Who else is in there?'

In the distance a siren rose and sank, but here the only sound was blown paper scratching the pavement. And our own voices.

'What about the tenant, the owner? Whoever told you about this place?'

'I don't know.'

'Aurelia! Who were you talking to?'

She turned; her face went stiff. 'You heard that?'

'Right. So?'

'It's a long story. Later.'

'Later, synonym for never.'

'No, really, later. There's no time! If Leo's really in there, we've can't just leave him there. We've got to do . . . something. Now!'

'Police?'

She shrank back.

'Never mind. They wouldn't have believed there was a problem when he disappeared. They're sure not going to believe me now, when I tell them he may possibly be in a house owned by somebody I don't know.'

'But we can't just walk away. If he's in there alone, if he's injured . . .' She sniffed back tears, swallowed and, for the first time, looked straight at me, pleading. 'He saved me! You don't know what it's like to lose everything. In prison you own nothing. Not even your body. Right or wrong; it makes no difference. You have nothing. *I* had nothing. My family was ashamed; any friends I thought I had vanished. No one came to see me. No one even asked to get on the list except Westcoff, and all he cared about was trying to implicate Leo. Only my mother wrote to me, and she was so righteous and furious and disappointed and God knows what that I would have been better off throwing out her letters without opening them. The only person who cared was Leo.' She swallowed again. 'Leo! I told him the first thing I'd do when I got out was come buy him dinner. Sometimes we talked about that – the dinner. I'd tell him where I'd take him: the Saint Francis, the Cliff House. I didn't know how little money you hit the street with.' Again she swallowed. 'Now . . . I haven't even gotten to see him at all!' As if in reaction, the siren wailed louder, nearer.

I'd had doubts about her and still had them, but this I believed. I glanced up at the building – flat surface, right against the protruding buildings on either side, two stories above us, two sliding windows on each, fire ladder in the middle. 'OK, let's do it.'

The door was a metal deal with two locks, both rusted. A door meant to stay shut, to keep out, not let in. Where a knock would be a warning. Even the EMTs or the cops, whoever was riding that siren, would have a hard time ramming through. And they weren't headed here.

I said, 'I want to check upstairs before I bang on the door and announce our presence. Give me a boost up to the fire escape.'

Fire escape was a compliment. How many decades had the rickety thing been hanging on for dear life? The bottom rung was ten or eleven feet up. 'Stand here. No, back a step. Just in front of the rung. Bend down, make a step with your hands and stand up. I'm going to step up on your shoulder and leap for it. Duck so I don't kick you. Can you do it?'

'For Leo? Sure.'

She bent down, clasped her hands.

I did not put my foot there. Instead I grabbed her by the shoulders. 'Tell . . . me . . . who's . . . in there! I'm not crashing through a window, making enough noise to alert everyone in the building and me not knowing what to find when you can just tell me! So who?'

'No one but Leo! I called a cell. He was on his way back. From downtown. He's going to be here any minute. I'll watch. I'll keep him here. He knows I'm coming. He won't suspect you're here. But you've got to move now!'

'Who, dammit! Westcoff?'

'Yeah.'

Maybe.

'He'll be here any minute!'

Leo or knowing; I had to choose.

She bent. I stepped into her hands, onto her shoulder and pushed off hard to leap for the rung. The rusty edge dug into my palms. I thrust a hand up to the next rung, and again. My skin burned. Toes against the building, I grabbed the next rung. The whole ladder shook. If I fell, I'd crack my skull.

Blocking out pain, I climbed hand over hand.

Flush against the wall there was barely space to wrap my fingers around the rungs. The metal rattled like wind chimes. Rubber toes pressing against the wall with each step, I counted on movement to save me. I flung myself over the edge of the roof just as the car passed.

Had the driver seen me? Was he even looking this way?

The car kept going. Not a police car. Not paramedics. Just a car. I didn't want to look at what I was lying in.

There had to be an entry from the roof. There was. I pushed up. Momentarily my hands stuck to the tar and gravel. It pulled on my shoes as I hurried across to the door and yanked.

Nothing.

The door did not move a whit.

I braced and pulled, but even as I did it I suspected that the door hadn't opened in a decade and definitely was not going to come ajar now.

The far side of the building was ten feet away, a wide air shaft. I peered over the edge into a black, dank hole.

How did people even get into this building? Was that one metal door the only entry? What ever happened to building regulations in this city!

More to the point, the only way I was going to find out if Leo was here was down that rusting excuse for a ladder, hanging off the side, peering into windows that were three feet away.

If he was *still* here. If I hadn't alerted his captor or captors. If they hadn't dragged him off somewhere else.

Or worse.

I crawled over, grabbed the rusted metal and braced to lower a foot over the edge.

Two cars rumbled down the alley ever more slowly as if the drivers were looking for something, or someone.

I waited on the flat tar roof. When they were both out of sight I lowered a foot over the edge onto the second rung. Grasping the rusty rungs had been treacherous climbing up, but going down was worse. Nothing was steady here, no rung reliable. My only option was to keep moving and hope the whole ladder didn't come loose from the stucco.

The windows were two-pane aluminum numbers, the kind that slide sideways. Cheap and flimsy. All to the good. I was level with the top edge on the upper of the two floors. Through the window to my right I could make out cardboard boxes piled haphazardly as if stuffed into a garage. The window on the left was so dirty it was hard to make out anything inside.

Because, I realized, there was nothing there. Just emptiness.

The rusty metal dug into my hands. My left foot had gone numb. I could barely feel it as I jammed the rubber shoe on the next rung.

An engine – car? truck? – was turning into the alley. There was nowhere to hide, to even hope for camouflage. I had to move! I near-rappelled, bouncing feet not on rungs but on the stucco, moving hand below hand on the sides of the ladder till I came even with the lower windows.

'Go!' Aurelia yelled.

'What?'

'I have to go . . . caught here . . . parole.' She didn't wait for me to respond. Shoes slapped the pavement.

The engine was nearer. I could drop, but I'd never get back up. And Leo . . .

'Aurelia?'

But she was gone. Gone so fast and far that I didn't even hear the slap of her shoes on the pavement.

When the going gets tough the tough get going . . . and fast.

Still, to be scooped back into prison . . . Could I blame her? Leo wouldn't.

The engine was louder.

I looked to my right through the window.

Then I saw it.

On the top of the sofa back, against the window.

Leo's kotsu.

His wooden teaching stick that had been at his side in the dokusan room. The stick his assailant had grabbed and beat him with.

It didn't mean Leo was here. Not even that he had been here. The last time I'd seen the kotsu it had been in his assailant's hand. Maybe it was just Hoodie inside.

No choice.

I grasped the edge of the ladder with both hands, pushed off and swung hard.

TWENTY-EIGHT

'Leo!'

'Super Woman!'

Glass was everywhere. The window had shattered, but I'd covered my face with my arms as I went through and now I grinned wide. 'You look good, really good.'

I surveyed the room. A clutch of filled-up cardboard cartons was passing as a bed, blankets, strewn newspapers, clutter, dust – everything streaked with dirt. And the smell of urine. But Leo looked OK. 'Are you—'

'Ready to leave. Hungry. Sore from kicking myself.'

'Things as they are,' I said, quoting one of the basic tenets of Zen Buddhism. We face things as they are.

He shot me the same look I'd aimed at Westcoff when he threw my practice in my face. Then he shrugged and said, 'Humble pie is a grisly meal. I just hope . . .'

'Hope later. We need to get out of here.'

He tried to get up and collapsed back onto the bed, his face pale, moist.

'When we get home I'll call a doctor.' I slipped an arm around his back and angled him up. 'Not Nezer, someone who's licensed in this state. If Gracie's back from her weird trip to Vegas . . .'

Not licensed in this state. I remembered now how I knew that. I stopped dead, realizing what it meant.

Which is how I heard the footsteps coming up the stairs.

The place was one room, for storage. No bathroom, no closet, not even a kitchen alcove. Nowhere to hide.

I lowered Leo to the floor behind a pile of boxes, grabbed a drop cloth, threw it on the bed and covered it with a dark towel. No one would think it was Leo, not for more than a moment.

A moment would be what I'd have.

The footsteps changed. He was on the landing now.

I looked around for a weapon. No bats, no metal rods, nothing but Leo's kotsu and I'd be damned if I'd use that.

Metal on metal. Key jammed into the lock.

I tiptoed across the room, braced myself against the wall beyond the door so he wouldn't hit me when he swung it open.

The door stuck momentarily. He shoved.

I braced my hands against the wall and kicked with every bit of fury I felt.

He groaned.

But my aim was off. Too high. I'd just knocked the wind out of him and he had enough strength to stagger back into the hall and pull the door shut.

I reached for the door to yank it open. Leo groaned softly. I wavered, then did the reasonable thing – flipped the security lock, pulled out my phone and called 911. Let the police go after Nezer Deutsch.

TWENTY-NINE

B y the time I got back to the production room I figured I could have written the script myself.
New Stunt Coordinator Explains Sudden Absence to Second Unit Director.

Me: Sorry I was gone. I've been involved in a kidnapping.

Beretski, not shifting his gaze from his notepad: Really?

Me: It was a police operation.

Beretski: Uh huh?

Me: I had no choice.

Him: Whatever.

How wrong I was. Beretski didn't bother to raise his voice. He sounded disappointed, exhausted and mutedly furious. 'That gag's got to be ready to roll at five a.m. no questions, no hold-ups. You don't have it ready, we don't shoot. If we don't shoot this gag, we don't have a movie. We couldn't wait if you had a note from God.'

'I—'

He leaned toward me, his head looming over mine. His breath smelled of junk food gone sour. 'I haven't slept in days. I thought I could count on you, that you could make this work. Before you took over coordinating I was overloaded but moving forward. You gave me an out. You know what I did? I slept! I lost eight hours in bed! Because I thought, I believed, you were taking over. Wrong! Now it's all back on me! I've got double the pressure. My head's throbbing so hard there should be brain splattered all over the room. I don't . . . I don't— Hell, I don't have time to waste on you.'

I didn't mention the digital adjustment I'd pushed, the thing that made it possible to get this gag done on schedule. I was history. I just scooped up my jacket and pack, walked out into the fog and left the shambles of my career behind.

I hadn't done it consciously but I'd made my choice: career or Leo.

* * *

'What other choice was there? Really?' I'd called for pizza from Leo's favorite North Beach establishment. We were in his room, he sitting cross-legged on his futon as he always did, me on a cushion on the floor, the open box of zucchini, black olive and double mushroom between us. The aroma of garlicy tomato sauce pervaded.

Leo looked better than he had in days. His color was normal, his eyes focused and the corners of his over-wide mouth looked ready to twitch into a grin. He extricated a piece and slid the box an inch toward me.

He took a bite from the wide end of the wedge, swallowed and said, 'Your sister Gracie called.'

'From Vegas?'

'The airport there.' Leo knew Gracie, my totally committed epidemiologist sister, the woman who believed the fate of our city hung solely on her vigilance against the armies of viruses, bacteria and germs crawling onto our beaches, flowing over our bridges, riding mass transit. Her assistant had told me Gracie had told her she was at a conference.

'Did she say what she was doing in Vegas?'

'Rafting down the Colorado River.'

'Gracie? She's never even taken the Ferry across the bay. To her water is what you use to clean your hands. How come she didn't tell us?'

'Maybe she didn't want to hear about water to wash away germs.'

'So she's home?'

'Not quite. She called from the airport in Las Vegas.'

'To tell me about rafting?'

'Not exactly. She said one of the women in the raft was looking feverish and she shifted to get a better look and—'

'Fell overboard?'

'''Fraid so. But that's not why she called. She hadn't packed her wallet where the guide told her.'

'Her wallet floated on down the Colorado River? It's probably clogging a spigot in Phoenix by now.'

'I bought her a ticket home.'

I laughed. That sounded like Gracie.

Career in shambles or not, it felt good to laugh. It felt great to be sitting on the floor in Leo's room, eating pizza, talking.

'There's nothing as wonderful as getting your life back.'

'This moment, all that exists.'

I nodded.

He hadn't said, 'If only I'd . . .' 'If only I hadn't done . . .' I was grateful.

I took another bite of pizza and chewed slowly, forming the question into words, realizing I was afraid to hear his answer. 'Do you remember *that moment*, the attack?'

'Some. Black hood; him rushing in. Grabbing my kotsu. That stunned me. And then him hitting me with it. Surreal.'

'Did you recognize him?'

'Physically? No. Maybe I did and the blows knocked it out of my head. But that's not quite what you're asking, is it?' He put his half-eaten slice back in the pizza box, shifted his legs into a more balanced position and turned to face me directly. 'I felt like it could be Nezer Deutsch. So maybe I did see a bit of his face and that got knocked out of my memory. But afterwards I couldn't be sure if I had seen anything at all or just had him on my mind because I'd heard from Aurelia, and I knew how much he felt she owed him. I'd been worried about her – that he might show up here trying to find her.'

'But then,' I prompted, 'you walked out of the hospital . . .'

'How could I lie around there? This is my temple, my people. I had to get back here and . . . and see. I guess I assumed—' He flashed a knowing smile as if to say, *How often have Zen masters insisted: Don't assume!*

'I couldn't just let the attacker wander around deciding what to do next. I had to figure this out – no one else was in any position to. I had a suspicion, but just that. I couldn't accuse Nezer. What if I was wrong? He'd already lost his license. Plus I had no proof. None.'

I raised my tea cup and took a sip before setting the issue between us. 'You suspected him and yet you insisted he come here.'

He put down his cup and looked not at but toward me in the openness of the space that connected us. 'He had to face me.'

'You did that for him?'

'I hoped for him. But I needed to be sure he was the one.'

'Were you?'

'Yes.'

'When?'

'Right before he jabbed a needle in my arm and dragged me out of here.' Then he shot me a grin. 'Maybe that wasn't the best time to confront him, huh?'

I reached for another slice of pizza. 'The police know who he is; it's only a matter of time till they find him. But if Deutsch does try something here we've got John's guard sitting in the courtyard. I got him a chair.' I leaned back against the wall and ate.

But Leo didn't move. 'I've had a lot of time to think, Darcy, to look at my own Buddhas, things as I want them to be, not as they are.

'It's a hard question: how do you balance security with freedom, with assumptions and reality, men and women. How do you balance compassion and safety? How far do you extend yourself for strangers? Who are strangers?'

'Yeah. And then there are members and regulars like Lila. We knew her but not really. I just hope she's OK. At least Sendar didn't get to follow her. He was too busy beating me up.'

Later, I would ask my teacher: where is our responsibility? Do we take sides? We who are told: do not judge by any standards? Now, though, I took a breath and broached the question I hadn't been able to ask. 'You said once you were sure you were right, and you were wrong. Was that about Aurelia?'

He nodded.

'You had to choose?'

He nodded again, slowly. 'A monastery up in marijuana country. I was desperate to be above suspicion. I was sure . . . I knew . . . I was wrong.'

'But she'd have gone to jail no matter what you did. She doesn't resent you turning her away. She adores you.'

A little smile he couldn't seem to restrain sneaked onto his face. 'Aurelia, yes. But Nezer, no. He blamed me then, he blames me now. If I had taken her in, maybe she wouldn't have been caught. Definitely she wouldn't have shown up at his door begging him to hide her. Then he wouldn't have believed she wanted to be with him, that she wasn't just looking for a place to hide.

Definitely he would not have been harboring a fugitive and he wouldn't have lost his license.'

'He blames you so he doesn't have to blame her? Like you said, "When you indulge your delusions, you create your own Buddha."'

Footsteps tapped up the stairs. I just about levitated off my cushion and spun toward the door. How could I have left the front door open? Today of all days?

THIRTY

'Aurelia!' Leo said. 'Come on in.' He smiled that sweet smile he had when Mom came to visit. Except this one was a little different.

Aurelia stood outside the doorjamb as if fearful of entering. For a moment I thought she was wary of me, guilty at abandoning me. But her gaze was on Leo, and the look of yearning disbelief and wonder was the same one I'd seen on Mom's face and felt on my own the day that my brother Mike came back from the missing.

'Give us a few minutes,' Leo said to me.

'You sure?' I couldn't keep myself from asking.

He was smiling too. 'I can handle her. Right, A?'

'Yeah.'

'I'll be back in half an hour,' I said, but I doubt either of them was listening.

It shouldn't have been a shock. Zen priests are not celibate. They have spouses, families, jobs, mortgages. Some priests live in Zen centers like Leo, but others could be the woman next door.

I walked down the stairs and out through the courtyard. The fog had never cleared and now at five p.m. it gave a rough charcoal coating to the sky and dripped that familiar wet somewhere between mist and drizzle. I should have grabbed a jacket. I didn't. I just walked.

Leo and I were never lovers. I'd never considered it. I felt sure he hadn't. He was like a brother, I'd told him, only without the eccentricities. With different ones, he'd corrected. And I'd had to agree. John might think nothing of planting a rent-a-cop in our courtyard, and Gary had threatened to take our landlord to the Supreme Court, but Leo had once been so deep into a dharma question he'd forgotten three meals in a row.

As I crossed Broadway the street seemed an out-of-focus backdrop of itself. The half-dark sky sucked up the strip club lights; the sidewalks were empty. It was 'before' time. Too early for dinner in North Beach, much too early for anything on Broadway.

They couldn't have been lovers before. But now? If Nezer Deutsch saw the look on her face he'd have no doubt.

Lovers? Or close, caring friends? I should have been happy for Aurelia. I was, I assured myself. And for Leo. Especially Leo, my friend. But for myself I felt hollow. 'I chose you! Over my career!' I muttered. A woman coming from the other direction moved away.

A cafe was opening. I slid in, ordered a glass of house red and sat, shivering a bit, sipping and feeling guilty for even having that thought. And foolish. And still empty.

I wanted to call someone for comfort, to assure me I hadn't lost both my career and the life I'd made at the zendo. To give me the illusion of comfort. Maybe that was the Buddha I should kill.

If you meet the Buddha in the road, kill the Buddha.

So I sat there with my loss. Life as it is, life as I didn't want it. And I felt a sudden pang of sorrow for Nezer Deutsch who had wanted Aurelia and lost his license.

I was overreacting, I knew. But sometimes you just need to do it. When I got back to the zendo I'd sit zazen and feel what I felt. Now, I finished my wine.

A while later I dialed the zendo phone where calls that automatically go to a voicemail were checked right away if we're there. 'Leo, if Aurelia'd like to stay tonight, it's fine with me.'

Leo was asleep when I got back, Aurelia in our 'guest' sleeping bag on my floor. She shook her head to wake herself, like a dog. 'You don't mind?'

'You don't snore?'

'Nope. It made me a super desirable roommate in camp. You know, Camp Bars-all-around?' She sat up, pulling the bag with her and clutching it under her arms. I had the sense she wanted to look away but it was almost impossible in this tiny room. 'I'm, uh, going to do the gag in the morning. Your gag.'

'It's OK.'

'You sure?'

'Sure as possible. I've gotten an appalling number of gigs when my predecessors broke limbs or ate bad fish. Stuff happens in stunt life. Nothing's the end. Dainen's furious, but in a while he'll forget. And then, AA, I'll have a buddy on the inside, right?'

'Of course. Of course,' she repeated, as if suddenly realizing she would truly be on the inside.

I was crawling into my own bedding when she told me Leo was going to lead zazen in the morning. 'It's supposed to be secret, but Renzo's going to be there. His niece called.'

'He's recovered enough?'

'Enough so the niece can't restrain him. Anyway, Leo said you should sleep in. You deserve it. He'll be fine.'

THIRTY-ONE

S leep in? With Aurelia Abernathy squeaking across the hall floor, banging the bathroom door as she tried to slip quietly inside in the four a.m. dark? Not hardly.

I padded downstairs and made strong tea for three, poured two servings into travel cups and slipped the third into Leo's room.

'You OK?' I asked him.

'Sterling.'

I hesitated. 'I'm worried—'

'Will I be safe? That's what you're asking?' He pushed up onto an elbow and shot me that grin that made me think: *Yeah, he's all right.* He said, 'You won't guess who else is coming here this morning. Quentin Snell.'

'Who? Oh, wait, you mean *Officer* Snell?'

'Correct. He said to tell you that you may have wondered why he seemed "cop out of water" – his term—'

'It was like he happened to wander up and stumble on a crime scene.'

'And so he did. Just back to work after a bad stretch, but off duty that day. He wasn't coming to a crime scene at all. He was hoping to learn to meditate.'

I must have looked skeptical. Leo added, 'And didn't your brother station an associate in the courtyard? I'll be doubly safe.'

By twenty after four, Aurelia and I stepped outside. The courtyard was damp and cold. The sky looked like it hadn't decided between fog and rain. I pulled up my hood, wrapped my scarf around my neck and, with a pang, passed John's buddy the cup of tea I'd made for myself. Aurelia was bouncing in place when I scooped up the *Chronicle* and slipped it in my pack.

'We're shooting from the top, up by Hyde, the first switch,' she said, taking long fast strides, drinking tea, the wind rustling her short, curly hair. 'Like you set up. First switch. Fourth switch. Dolly on ropes so it's barely moving.'

I nodded, not that she noticed as we hurried north on Columbus. Just as well. I had spent hours pondering how to create the illusion of movement, of going from balance to near loss of control while the dolly was moving slowly enough so the grips could keep it under control. In the end I'd gone with the low-tech motion management method. 'Are you using two ropes?'

'Right. I practiced. It'll work great. They're going to use only one rope for the last switch, so they can swing the dolly more. Cool, huh?'

My gag, the one *I* created, that I had assumed *I* would be doing. I could almost feel the dolly under me just thinking about the gags.

If you meet the Buddha on the way, kill the Buddha. My ticket to success; my Buddha? I swallowed and said, 'After the first two switches, you'll be an old pro. You can give that last one a shimmy.'

By the time we climbed the stair-step sidewalk to the top of Lombard, things had shifted for me. Maybe it was the hour, the all-out walk, the prospect of coffee, but I was anxious just to see the gags be a go.

'I've been up all night, thanks to you!' the wardrobe mistress grumbled at one or both of us. 'Had to take in every outfit.'

The head of the grounds crew, who'd had to remind Aurelia about the hydrangeas in the outcroppings, wasn't pleased with me, on general principles, it seemed. And when I spotted one guy I'd worked with on lighting, I made it my business to grab a coffee and ease back into the shadows. When you create angst on the set, no one's your friend.

The narrow sidewalks were packed, as if every onlooker who had endured the mornings of wait and watch and see next to nothing had gotten out here for the payoff and invited ten of their friends. They lined the steps, some in slickers, some bare-headed in zipped-up jackets. Even in the pre-dawn light the green, red and yellow slickers covering heads and shoulders had a festive look.

It surprised me how few of the gaffers and grips I actually knew. I'd thought I'd talked to everyone. The actress, whose body was more similar to mine than Aurelia's, showed up just before the first take, and I avoided her.

The dolly was four foot square, fourteen inches high. Grips looped ropes, the same red as the brick roadway, over the back two wheels. They were burly guys, and squatting, holding, almost sitting on the curbs, they seemed to have no problem guiding and shifting the dolly as smoothly as if it was on a track. After it had gone two feet, Aurelia leapt on, braced, knees bent, back rounded, arms out. She looked, for all the world, like she was flying down the steep switchback, just in slow mo.

When she jumped off, everyone applauded. Softly. No matter how good she was, this was still seven-thirty on a Monday morning.

She beamed.

For her, I thought, there would never be another moment as good as this.

I was wrong. She was even better on the second switchback. She managed a quaver to her arms, fingers taut and clawed out as if grabbing air. When she leapt off no one worried about being noisy. Crew and cast, cops and neighbors, everyone cheered. Dainen Beretski all but hoisted her on his shoulders.

'You're a natural!' I called out to her.

'Hey you did the set-up. I just went along for the ride!'

Not true, but nevertheless nice.

Some of the gaffers and grips were already carrying the camera-dolly tracks downhill. The lighting crew was checking near the bottom of the street, and Margo, the continuity woman, was all but jumping out of her skin urging them to hurry before the sun came out. *As if*, I thought with a glance at the sky. The wardrobe mistress was close-eyeing Aurelia's dress for specks and tears, pulled threads, any marks that might magnify on film.

It was all I could do not to rush down to oversee the angles of the banks of lights, double-check the pitch of the switchback elbows. Extras clumped on the sidewalks. Dainen had planned to use them another day, but now everything had to be a wrap this morning. There'd be clean-up shots after Aurelia's third gag. Then it would be pack the trucks and bye bye.

I slipped back into the lunch wagon, pushing between extras and neighbors, snagged another coffee, ate half a croissant, told myself the sensible thing would be to go back to the zendo and make sure Leo was all right on his first morning leading zazen, as opposed to standing around here for the eternity it would take to set up this last shot. But, of course, I didn't. I sipped the coffee, pulled the *Chronicle* out of my pack and opened it with the air of someone doing exactly what she'd planned for her morning.

'Wow!' I said aloud. There, below the fold on page one was a picture of Lila Suranaman. Next to it was a headline: *Human Trafficking, an Insider's Tale.* Byline: Roman Westcoff. Lila was pictured so clearly it made me sure she was somewhere safe.

I'd read it later – maybe take it to Renzo's after zazen.

Unable to restrain myself, I walked down to the bottom of the street. Lombard switches back and forth eight times and shoots south onto Leavenworth. This final part of the gag would take in the last two curves. The dolly was already in place at the top of the two, the rope holding it attached to a hook nestled under the center back. I had considered hooking it at a corner but decided against that – not enough control. Still I – *they* – had two big guys on the holding end.

Aurelia trotted down the street, not on a sidewalk but taking the middle of the bricked roadway, as close to running as she could without flying head over heels. She eyed the dolly.

Then she spotted me and veered over.

'If you grin any wider, you'll break your ears,' I said.

'Worth it!' She lowered her voice. 'I dreamed of this every day I was inside, but, you know, I couldn't have imagined *this!* I—' Her voice caught.

'Hey, make-up! Don't run your mascara!'

She laughed at the stunt woman in-joke – the face that's never seen – slapped my shoulder and bounced into the roadway.

It was already eight-thirty a.m. There was no way they'd get the fill shots done. But that wasn't my problem.

Aurelia leapt onto the dolly. The guys jiggled it and she balanced. Dainen called for silence and the crowd noise turned off. Everyone was holding his breath.

'Action!'

They eased the dolly slowly, jerkily now with only the one rope holding it, down the incline toward the first of these two elbows. Aurelia bent left, leaning far over the edge of the dolly as it started right into the curve.

She's good! Really good! When they sped up the film in post-production she'd look like she was doing fifty miles per hour. When she saw the dailies she'd be proud.

The dolly rounded the steeply banked elbow. Aurelia was squatting so low her head almost touched the wood. She'd been holding the pose forever. Her thighs had to be burning. She'd be sore tonight. The soreness of triumph.

Slowly, the dolly came into the straight roadway between the two elbows and she eased back up, arms flinging slowly up toward the sky. The dolly was shaking; her legs were shaking; she was smiling as the dolly eased toward us, into the last elbow and she leaned forward toward the cross street, the end.

He came out of nowhere. Rammed her in the back.

She flew off the dolly, above the roadway, onto the pavement on Leavenworth.

Onto her head.

The crowd was dead silent.

She made no sound.

The only voice was his, Nezer Deutsch's as he ran to her, bent beside her dead and broken body. 'I'm a doctor! I'll take care of her. She's mine. Mine!'

If you meet your *Buddha in the road . . .*